Stud Finder

Also From Lauren Blakely

The Seductive Nights Series
First Night (Julia and Clay, prequel novella)
Night After Night (Julia and Clay, book one)
After This Night (Julia and Clay, book two)
One More Night (Julia and Clay, book three)
A Wildly Seductive Night (Julia and Clay novella, book 3.5)
Nights With Him (A standalone novel about Michelle and Jack)
Forbidden Nights (A standalone novel about Nate and Casey)

The Sinful Nights Series
Sweet Sinful Nights
Sinful Desire
Sinful Longing
Sinful Love

The Fighting Fire Series
Burn For Me (Smith and Jamie)
Melt for Him (Megan and Becker)
Consumed By You (Travis and Cara)

The Jewel Series
A two-book sexy contemporary romance series
The Sapphire Affair
The Sapphire Heist

Stud Finder

By Lauren Blakely

1001 Dark Nights

EVIL EYE
CONCEPTS

Stud Finder
By Lauren Blakely

1001 Dark Nights

Copyright 2017 Lauren Blakely
ISBN: 978-1-945920-23-3

Foreword: Copyright 2014 M. J. Rose

Published by Evil Eye Concepts, Incorporated

Acknowledgments from the Author

I'm grateful to so many people who are bringing this book to you. First and foremost, thank you to Liz Berry and MJ Rose for the amazing opportunity to be part of 1001 Dark Nights. Big thanks to KP Simmon for daily support, strategy, and encouragement. Thank you to Helen Williams for finding the lovely cover images. On the editorial side, I am fortunate to lean on Lauren Clarke, Kim Bias, Dena Marie and Jen McCoy for story guidance, and to Tiffany for eagle eyes. Thank you to Kelley, Candi and Keyanna for the day to day work that is so vital. As always, thank you to readers for making dreams come true.

Sign up for the 1001 Dark Nights Newsletter
and be entered to win a Tiffany Key necklace.

There's a contest every month!

Go to www.1001DarkNights.com to subscribe.

As a bonus, all subscribers will receive a free
1001 Dark Nights story
The First Night
by Lexi Blake & M.J. Rose

One Thousand and One Dark Nights

Once upon a time, in the future…

*I was a student fascinated with stories and learning.
I studied philosophy, poetry, history, the occult, and
the art and science of love and magic. I had a vast
library at my father's home and collected thousands
of volumes of fantastic tales.*

*I learned all about ancient races and bygone
times. About myths and legends and dreams of all
people through the millennium. And the more I read
the stronger my imagination grew until I discovered
that I was able to travel into the stories… to actually
become part of them.*

*I wish I could say that I listened to my teacher
and respected my gift, as I ought to have. If I had, I
would not be telling you this tale now.
But I was foolhardy and confused, showing off
with bravery.*

*One afternoon, curious about the myth of the
Arabian Nights, I traveled back to ancient Persia to
see for myself if it was true that every day Shahryar
(Persian: شهريار, "king") married a new virgin, and then
sent yesterday's wife to be beheaded. It was written
and I had read, that by the time he met Scheherazade,
the vizier's daughter, he'd killed one thousand
women.*

*Something went wrong with my efforts. I arrived
in the midst of the story and somehow exchanged
places with Scheherazade — a phenomena that had
never occurred before and that still to this day, I
cannot explain.*

Now I am trapped in that ancient past. I have taken on Scheherazade's life and the only way I can protect myself and stay alive is to do what she did to protect herself and stay alive.

Every night the King calls for me and listens as I spin tales. And when the evening ends and dawn breaks, I stop at a point that leaves him breathless and yearning for more. And so the King spares my life for one more day, so that he might hear the rest of my dark tale.

As soon as I finish a story... I begin a new one... like the one that you, dear reader, have before you now.

Prologue

Once upon a time, in a wonderfully romantic land known as Manhattan, there was a woman who possessed a particular skill. She had the uncanny ability to match—clothes and colors, food and wine, and most importantly, people. She was so skilled that she was sought out far and wide across the city by those seeking to find their true soul mate.

At the same time, there was a most handsome man who was brilliant, funny, and, let's call a spade a spade, a wee bit socially clueless.

Fine. More than a bit. Perhaps, a lot. But he was a hot nerd, and his brain worked quite well for everything else, and he was in demand as a mate.

He was also ready to settle down, and because he had learned to depend on machines, he was certain a machine would find his true love for him.

When the woman heard of such an insane notion, she could simply not abide by it. She made him an offer to show him how to find a match in real life, without relying on an algorithm. Because he was a natural risk-taker, he gave her three chances to prove what she could do.

Determined to help find him true love, she took on this challenging assignment. Even though she found him handsome, and even though, for the first time ever, she felt the faintest stir of attraction for a client, she bore no risk of that admiration turning into something else. Both online and in the real world, the man and woman could agree that opposites didn't attract at all. And who could ever fall for someone with such a vastly different view of life and love?

But things are not always what they seem…

Chapter One

Dylan

The Internet and I are best friends. We've done everything together. We've grown up together. We've downloaded music, we've ordered food, we've learned new languages, we've discovered women, and we've made millions.

As I turn toward the entrance for Chelsea Piers on a Friday afternoon, my phone in my hand, I see no reason why I can't find a woman here.

Not Chelsea Piers.

Please.

Who meets people in person anymore?

That's crazy talk.

I mean *here*. On this fantastic device I'm holding. This is where everyone finds love these days. Swiping left, swiping right. Hitting this button. Liking that button. Okay fine, maybe they're finding other things. But I'm determined to discover happiness the same way I've discovered everything else. *Online*.

"This ad is a winner." I brandish my phone at Mia, one of my closest friends, and my teammate on my laser tag team when she's in town. "Any second now, I will be this much closer to finding Mrs. Right, don't you think?"

Her hazel eyes stare intently at the screen, and her answer comes in the form of a perfectly arched eyebrow. "Wow. That's pretty much on the nose."

I reach the door and yank it open, a blast of cool air conditioning greeting us. "Isn't it best for me to go all in? Why fuck around?"

She laughs. "I suppose because perhaps not revealing *all* your cards at once can be a good thing when it comes to dating."

I scoff. "No need to hold back. I'm ready for the real thing." I push my glasses higher up on the bridge of my nose. "Besides, don't you know me by now? Do I do anything half-baked?"

"You're usually fully roasted." She places a hand on my arm. "But don't you honestly want to try a softer touch? Maybe hold a little something back?"

As we stride to the check-in counter, ready to tackle all forms of entrepreneur enemies in our weekly CEO club game, I shake my head. "Look, the great thing about the Internet is you can be completely direct. You can say exactly what you want. It's not like when you meet somebody in person and have to worry about following the right protocol, saying the right thing, discussing or not discussing the right topic. When you find someone online, you can 100 percent be yourself and speak the truth. So that's what I do."

Besides, this is The. Best. Ad. Ever.

Man seeks woman:

Hot, rich, smart, witty, self-made multimillionaire Internet genius seeks classy, intelligent, sexy, fun-loving woman who's interested in new experiences and sharing all the good things, from eating out, to movies, to softball, to savoring the adventure of this amazing world together.

Who wouldn't answer that ad?

"Let me get this straight," Mia says as the attendant hands us our weapons and we head into the laser tag arena, ready to save Gotham from the bad guys. "Do you think everyone is speaking the truth online?"

I laugh as I take off my Yankees ball cap and set it in a locker. I turn off my phone and tuck it in the hat. "That's not what I'm saying. What I am saying is there is no empirical evidence that meeting someone IRL"—I stop to sketch air quotes—"improves your chances at love."

"Nor is there evidence that meeting someone online improves your chances."

"You met Patrick in person, and you're not even a thing yet," I say, mentioning the guy she's been keen on for some time.

She shakes her head at me, her eyes turning to slits. "You know that's *not* the reason we're not a thing."

I wave a hand. "Too many *nots* in that sentence."

"Just wait and see if I cover for you in today's game."

"You will. Because you're just as competitive as I am. And speaking of, let's wager. If I don't find Mrs. Right waiting for me on my phone at the end of this game, I'll buy drinks tonight for the whole crew."

She offers a hand to shake. "Deal."

Then I race through the darkened cityscape, ducking behind cardboard buildings, hiding behind cutouts of bridges as I mow down a pack of app-making CEOs. We emerge victorious at the end of our hour-long session. I'm both ready for a round of drinks, no matter who's treating, and prepared to check out the bounty of beautiful, brilliant babes who are also eager to find true love.

I turn my phone on as I leave with Mia, ready to meet up with our buddies. "What do you think? Will we find the next Mrs. Parker here?" I ask, tapping the screen.

"Oh yeah. Absolutely. She'll be the one wearing an apron and waving to you from in front of a white picket fence."

I stop in my tracks when I open the inbox on the dating site. It's clogged. I stare at my phone, as if something's wrong with it. "It's like it's all backed up," I say, as if this is a math problem I can't solve.

Mia tugs her blond hair out of her ponytail holder. "Oh, really? I'm so shocked. Do you mean ten thousand women answered your ad?"

My jaw comes unhinged as I stare at the cornu-*un*-copia of messages. Men, women, mail-order brides, women with teeth, women without teeth, thrice-divorced ladies, women in knee-high socks and short shorts with breasts the size of potted plants, as well as girls who look like they haven't even graduated high school.

I swallow and gulp. Maybe I was a little off with my prediction. "It's like it's teeming with the masses."

Mia sighs and smiles. "That's the problem."

Chapter Two

Evie

You just know when some things go together.

And I know this adorable and badass teal leather skirt will pair perfectly with my friend Olivia's scarf. Plus, hello. This skirt is less than forty dollars. Can you say deal? Come to Mama.

I zoom in on the skirt, snatching it from the shelves and wielding it like a prize. "Olivia, this would go amazingly with your coral scarf," I tell my client and friend. "The light silky one."

She gives me a quizzical look from across the rack at the consignment shop in the Village I've scoured today. "Are you sure, Evie?"

"Have I ever led you astray?" I ask, eyeing her engagement ring. It's a stunning emerald cut, and I helped her fiancé, a deliciously hot vet— *meow*—pick it out for her.

"Never, ever. But are you sure? Turquoise and coral?"

I count off on my fingers. "Turquoise and coral. Purple and gray. Pink and yellow. They're beyond blue and orange, and red and black. They're unexpected combos. Like a hacker and a vet."

I could color match by the time I was six. I could pick outfits with an uncanny ease and sense of fashion. Over the years, that keen sense of pairing evolved from the chocolate-goes-with-strawberry variety to this-man-will-fall-madly-for-this-woman.

Olivia is one of my people, a brunette, green-eyed, blissfully-in-love ethical hacker who's paid gobs to break into bank security. Earlier this year, I linked her up with a smoldering and ridiculously fit vet on the Upper East Side who handles all the teacup chihuahuas and poodles in the city, it seems.

"I'm buying the skirt as a gift. Wear it to the upcoming gallery opening."

"Herb and I can't wait for the event," she says.

See? That's one of the ways I knew she and her beau would be perfect together. They share a deep and abiding passion for art installations—the weirder the better—and that's what I've found the online dating sites of the world disregard. What's under the surface in a match. Like his name. His parents saddled him with one of the worst names in the world to give a modern man. *Herbert* is just, well, it's a turn-off. But I knew Olivia would look beneath the surface. That's what she does for a living. That's what she does with people, too, and now they're slated to marry in a few more months.

She grabs a trucker hat from a shelf, the mesh variety with a silhouette of a woman on the front. She positions it jauntily mere inches above her pretty brown hair. "Perfect for my next business meeting?"

My blue eyes turn to daggers. "Don't. Lower. Your. Arms."

She laughs. "I wasn't going to actually put it on."

I breathe again. "Good. I can't help myself, though. I see a hat near a friend's head, and all my training kicks into gear."

"Anti-lice training?"

"Yes. Exactly," I say, as if it's a joke, though truth be told, it is not a joke. I wear a scarf on my head at theaters to protect my blond locks, I travel on planes wearing a hooded sweatshirt, and I never, ever rest my head on anyone else's pillow.

It's just better to be safe than scratchy-headed.

"I should get this for my brother, though. Once, you know, I've sanitized it in a vat of color-safe bleach."

"Does he like mesh trucker hats with hot chicks on them?"

She eyes the hat suspiciously and sets it down. "Come to think of it, no. I'm just tired of seeing a New York Yankees hat on him all the time."

I point at the mesh hat as I consider a black lace vintage skirt. "I'm not sure that's an improvement, though. Wait. Which brother are we talking about? The hot nerd or the hotter nerd?"

She laughs, then sticks out her tongue. "Can we please not refer to any of my brothers as hot?"

"Even though that's what half of New York City calls them?"

Olivia's brothers are gorgeous identical-twin tech multimillionaires. I know them both from the softball league my brother, Patrick, convinced me to join. Though, to be fair, *join* is a euphemism for my role. Due to an extreme allergy to competitive sports in any way, shape, or form, I don't actually play softball. Instead, I manage the team. But that suits my organizational heart much better than digging my heels in at home plate and trying to whack a ball whizzing too fast near my face.

"As I'm sure you can imagine, I still think of my brothers—both of them—as complete and utter ding-dongs," she says as we walk to the counter. "Case in point. Dylan put an ad online yesterday, looking for his soulmate. He's such a doofus."

My skin prickles, like spiders are crawling down my spine. "LIKE ON TINDER?"

Oops. I think I just spoke in shouty caps.

Look, I'm not technically opposed to hookup sites. I *get* that they fill a certain human need. A primal urge, you might say. But the problem is, they've numbed men and women from taking their time to get to know someone and finding real love.

"It was something else. I'm trying to remember."

"Please say it was an elite matchmaking online site where the registrants need to pay fees in the triple digits at least," I add, worry in my tone. Even though I'm a professional matchmaker, I can coexist quite nicely with my online counterparts that actually require a certain degree of vetting.

Olivia winces, and a heavy sigh follows. "It was one of those plenty-of-sharks-in-the-sea places."

"No!" I am the Wicked Witch, melting. I snap my gaze from the rack of vintage skirts on my right to the cute Peter Pan dresses on my left, hoping I didn't actually scream that out loud.

"'Fraid so," Olivia says, confirming my worst professional fears.

I press my hands together in prayer. "Say it isn't so. Say you're teasing. Say you're pulling my leg."

Olivia grabs her phone and shows me the ad.

With each line, I wither inside. I park my hands on her shoulders. "I implore you. For the love of all that is good and holy, for all the women in the world, we can't let him do this."

"Why?" Her voice seems laced with genuine surprise. "Dylan is a master at all things online. He lives and dies by the Web."

"Two words. *Gold digger.* He's going to be besieged with women, and he's too sweet to know what hit him. He'll be like a puppy dog. You see what it's like at softball games. Sometimes women are there checking out both of your brothers."

She sneers. "And he still thinks the women at softball are cheering him on for hitting a home run. He's competitive like that."

"My point precisely. He'll be swarmed with catfishers. Your brother is ridiculously rich and completely clueless and adorably hot."

She screws up the corner of her mouth. "That does kind of describe Dylan to a T, minus the adorably hot part. But what are we supposed to do?"

"Help him," I say, pleading. "This is like Wonder Woman walking past the wounded. She can't leave them behind."

She blinks. "But your clientele is women. You're the Stud Finder."

"My clientele is *mostly* women," I correct. "Because that's who usually comes to a matchmaker. But darling, I have to know the men, too. How else would I have paired you with Herb the hot vet?"

She smiles, her straight white teeth gleaming. "I do love my Herb."

As the Stud Finder, I help well-off single women in Manhattan find men who won't fleece them—men who will love and cherish them. I've made a fantastic living, thank you very much, with my eyes. That sense of color matching? My fashion skills? My knowledge of personalities? I parlayed that into a psychology degree, a career as an executive recruiter, and now I use it as the head of an elite matchmaking business. I'm outgoing, I speak my mind, and I know nearly everyone in New York City. I've become the shield, the sword, and the lubricant for dozens of women to find their Mr. Right.

That's because I don't go for the obvious matches.

Forget the football player and the cheerleader, the beauty and the beast, the virgin and the billionaire. My skills lie in finding subtler combinations and unexpected pairings. The philanthropist and the man who photographs dogs for rescue organizations, the magazine editor and the venture capitalist, the best-selling romance novelist and the hot, young comedian who makes her laugh.

Those are my couplings.

While I have very little in common with Dylan Parker, I can appreciate all he brings to the table. And that's why, even though my clients are usually women, I know I have to help him. I simply can't let a man who's that much of a catch take this sort of risk.

"I volunteer as tribute." I raise a hand high. "I will find the perfect woman for your brother." The Stud Finder will become a Studette Searcher.

"I'll run it past him to make sure he's game, and I'd love to pay for your services."

I furrow my brow and shake my head. "Your money is no good here. It's my gift to you. An engagement gift," I say with a wink.

She drops her hand to my arm. "Evie, you don't have to do that. I'm more than happy to pay. He's my brother, after all, no matter how challenging the case is."

I laugh. "All the more reason for me to do it pro bono. It'll sharpen my skills to handle tough cases."

"Then I suspect he'll have an even harder time saying no. He can't turn down a deal."

Nor can I when it comes to clothes. I buy the skirt for Olivia, and that cute black one? I grab it on the way out, and plunk down twenty-two dollars. That is one hell of a steal.

Chapter Three

Dylan

Dylan: Yo.

    Ryder: What's up?

    Dylan: My sister wants me to use a matchmaker.

    Ryder: Your sister is brilliant.

    Dylan: That's it? That's all?

    Ryder: Did you want a lengthy explanation? Or should I let you know I'm still laughing at the ad you posted?

    Ryder: Did you post it for my amusement? If so, well done.

    Ryder: Also, seriously. I feel responsible for this. Have I not done my best to train you and your brother in the ways of being rich, single, and in demand in New York City?

    Dylan: Sorry, I can't hear you over the sarcasm and mockery.

    Ryder: I only mock you because you're mockable.

    Dylan: And I thought my sister was mean…

    Ryder: You ain't seen nothing yet.

    Ryder: But seriously, man. I get it. I understand where you're coming from. I also agree that you might benefit from someone to separate the wheat from the chaff. Do what Olivia says.

    Dylan: All right. The master has spoken.

    Ryder: Orders straight from the Consummate Wingman.

* * * *

I move the knight two squares over, then up. "So she's doing this out of the goodness of her heart?"

Olivia peers at the chessboard in front of us in Washington Square Park. Without raising her gaze from the board, she answers, "She likes me, and she also sees it as her civic duty to help you."

I laugh as I run a hand through hair that's in need of a trim. "I'm her charity case?"

Olivia raises her face and winks, her green eyes the same shade as mine. "Dylan, don't you know? You're always the charity case. Comes with being the youngest." She moves her rook.

"But I'm also the smartest," I say as I capture her rook on my next move. I dangle the chess piece in the warm summer air. "Ha!"

"Foiled again," she says, cursing.

"Anyway, you really think I should use a matchmaker? I'll admit I considered it briefly when you used one, but it just seemed like the Internet had to be a better solution."

"Can we agree now that the Internet *wasn't* the better solution for you?"

I take a beat, reflecting back on the responses I received from my ad. None were from women who were "interested in new experiences and sharing all the good things," but rather those who wanted to experience my bank account and share my wallet.

"Fine. At first glance, the ad didn't entirely pan out. But you think this woman can find *the one*?"

Olivia shrugs casually. "I do think she can. I found Herb through her," she says, wagging her left hand at me.

A cone of light from her diamond nearly blinds me. "I can't see anymore!"

She laughs. "Exactly. Listen, to use your favorite analogy—it's a no-harm, no-foul situation."

I mime dunking a basketball.

"If you had any athletic talent, you'd have been dangerous," she says.

"Ah, but I bet I would have made an excellent polo player," I say, adopting a snooty accent.

She snorts. "Oh, too right. You'd have been bloody brilliant on a horse."

"Also, don't forget, I'm still fast, and I'm excellent at softball."

She nods slowly. "Right. Slow-pitch softball. We're all good at that,

Dylan."

I toss my hands up, exasperated. "And why do I listen to you?"

She stretches her arm to pinch my cheek. "Because you're adorable, and you need help. Evie will help you. She's sharp, direct, and fun. And listen, I wouldn't feel right letting you go out on dates with women you meet from an ad. I know your friend Ryder would say the same thing."

I nod. "True, that. In fact, he already did. So did Mia. The level of mockery she put me through was pretty intense on the Sarcasm Scale."

"What are we waiting for then?"

"For me to win this game," I say, sliding my queen toward her king at the edge of the board. "Checkmate."

She scowls.

I park my hands behind my head. "It's so satisfying beating you. Like, incredibly, absolutely, fantastically satisfying."

"It was satisfying when I beat you up when you were a scrawny kid, too."

"You never beat me up. Not once."

She glances at her watch. "So much for me helping you find the woman of your dreams," she says, and rises as if she's about to dart off.

I grab her wrist. "Liv, you gave the most painful noogies when you were a kid, and I still have bruises on my skull to prove your strength."

She smiles wickedly. "That's what I thought. Anyway, why don't you and Evie meet tomorrow? She has a tight schedule, but I can probably convince her to fit you in to grab a coffee and chat. She likes coffee. Correction—she *loves* coffee."

I groan. "She's one of those coffee snobs? They're so hard to take."

"You're a tea snob."

"Because tea is awesome. It's classy. It's unconventional. But everyone likes coffee."

She flings her hands in the air. "Fine. How about boba tea?"

I crinkle my nose. "I'm a tea lover. Boba tea is like an affront to my senses, whether someone calls it boba tea or bubble tea." I shudder.

"Perhaps try it then, snob. There's a boba tea shop that makes the drinks by machine. You place an order and these robotic arms make it."

My eyes widen. "I like the sound of that."

"I thought you might. You guys can review all the details over your robotically-crafted tea balls."

Chapter Four

Evie

Quickie.

I'm meeting him at a place called Quickie.

I shake my head, amused and baffled that a store would choose such a name. I stare at the orange sign and squint as if the letters will rearrange themselves into something that doesn't suggest an afternoon romp.

Not that I have anything against afternoon romps. Though, truth be told, it's been a while since I had a romp at any hour of the day. Afternoon, evening, or morning.

I'm a big fan of romping, but the sad reality is I've been too busy with building my business to have time.

Ironic, because I tell my clients we always make time for the things we want. Lord knows, I make plenty of time to hunt out bargains at the best vintage and consignment shops all around Manhattan, and I post them on my blog for fun.

But I haven't made time for the dating that would lead to romping since business has been my top priority.

It still is, which is why I'm here at Quickie, since helping Dylan will make me an even better matchmaker. I'm ten minutes early because I don't believe in arriving late. Ever.

As I wait on the sidewalk outside the shop, I partake in one of my favorite activities—watching people.

I craft stories as I scan the block. Cruising past me in sky-high heels, a rail-thin woman barks into her phone about picking up a dress from the tailor. What event is she attending? Is the dress for her? Is she having the hem hiked up or the waist taken in? Does she want to look sexy for an ex or proper for work?

"And make sure the neckline plunges an extra inch," she instructs.

Sexy for an ex.

Next, I spot a businessman scurrying into a black Honda with a pink mustache sign on the dash. He holds the door for a pig-tailed, pip-squeak blonde in a yellow poufy dress.

Weekend-working dad is taking a break from the office to take his daughter to a princess party.

A tall guy with muscly, ropy arms on display in a blue tee enters my line of vision. The soft faded jeans show off a great ass. The kind you can grab onto while he pounds you.

Whoa? Where the hell did that dirty thought come from?

I shake my head, chasing it away, as I resume my inventory.

That shirt makes it dead clear he has a flat stomach. I slide into my happy zone of admiration for a moment, because he truly possesses a fantastic body. The trouble is he's wearing a ball cap, and his head is bent over his phone.

I frown as I write his story. *Hipster dude, unable to interact with the world.* It's not that hard to put your phone away, guy.

He lifts his face, and I blink.

Then I admonish myself.

I should absolutely not be admiring the body of my new client.

Not. At. All.

I conduct a full mind sweep as I wave at Dylan, affixing the most cheery, chipper matchmaker face I possibly can. The I-was-not-checking-out-your-ass look.

I've known Dylan for the last year or so. He's our first baseman, and a Scrabble teammate in a monthly competition hosted by some friends, not to mention the winner of the Punniest Costume from Olivia's most recent Halloween party, put on by her friend Henley at the Battery Park penthouse she shares with her fiancé, Max. Sporting a blue shirt, Dylan had draped a phone cord around his neck and hung a rubber chicken from it for Chicken Cord on Blue.

How have I never noticed his ass before? Maybe I was looking at the chicken. Although, in all fairness, I think I checked out his behind on the field in Central Park when he whacked a grand slam earlier this summer.

I wave. "Hi, Dylan!"

He stops a foot away from me. "Hey, Evie, person who's not holding a cell phone like everyone else in the city. How do you function?"

I laugh. "I know. I'm a throwback."

"And it's not even TT. Throwback Thursday," he says, quickly explaining. "You're old-school interacting with the RW." He pauses, peering at me through his brown eyeglasses. "That's real world."

"I figured as much."

He laughs awkwardly. "Sorry. I get caught up." He steps closer and offers a hand to shake. He stops. Shakes his head. "Wait. That's weird. We can hug, right?"

A smile crosses my lips. "We can definitely hug IRL."

He laughs again, and this time it's not awkward.

As he wraps his arms around me, he says, "I was debating a cheek kiss, but that seemed old-fashioned. Same as a kiss on the hand. By the way, did my sister tell you she thinks I'm socially clueless?"

I don't answer him right away, because his arms are so sturdy, stronger than I'd expected, and I'd nearly forgotten how tall he was—I'm guessing six foot one. And he smells so good, like deodorant, which is actually quite a nice scent on a man since it means he's showered, and he's clean.

I'm a big fan of clean.

As surreptitiously as I can, I draw a subtle inhale, savoring the fresh smell before we separate. "There's nothing wrong with socially clueless. I believe we've all got a bit of a dork in us."

He arches an eyebrow and eyes me from stem to stern. "Fine, where's your dork? Because I don't believe it. You're perfectly put together." His green eyes roam over me, taking in my new black lace skirt that hits at the knee—it's springy and fun, but not, ya know, vaginal-length, like far too many skirts are. I've paired it with a lavender short-sleeve top, with little silver studs down the side stitches. On my feet are Mary Janes. Which are the perfect shoes—chunky heeled for comfort and adorable for fashion.

"Also, that's a cute skirt," he adds.

I can't help myself. I have to price brag. "Twenty-two dollars at Audrey's Closet. I found it on the back rack, and I couldn't resist."

He offers a hand to high-five. "Score. Next time, you'll be telling me you have a Groupon for boba tea." He wiggles his eyebrows in mock excitement.

"I wish."

He points. "You're a bargain hunter."

"Sometimes. And to answer your question about my inner dork, I have one in me since this"—I run my finger along the bottom of my chin, highlighting my scar—"is why I don't look at my phone on the streets."

He peers at the faded blue line on my chin. "You have a cell phone wound. I've heard of people who trip and fall while looking at their phones, but I've never met such a rare breed of person."

I jut my hip out and curtsy. "Now you have, and it was no ordinary trip and fall."

He presses his palms together in plaintive prayer. "I must know every gory detail."

Chapter Five

Dylan

Walking and tweeting, jogging and Facebooking, and running and emailing all require a particular type of focus. I'm not saying I'm a pro at that sort of multitasking. Not at all.

But I do enjoy a good cell phone mishap tale. "Let me guess."

She parks her hands on her hips, saying *go for it*.

I study her, tapping my finger against my bottom lip, as if I can discern how she might have landed on a YouTube compilation of cell phone mishaps. Then I find myself distracted because Evie is an interesting combination of cute and sexy—she has a perfectly put-together look to her with her shampoo-commercial hair and her outlined lips, but her clothes are fun, and even though they're completely appropriate, they don't hide the tight, trim figure she has.

Her legs are muscular, her waist is trim, and her breasts are small, but firm. She has a certain blue-eyed, fair-haired bubbliness, like you might run into her on Rodeo Drive with a chihuahua poking its head out of an expensive handbag on her arm. But instead, she's a New Yorker through and through, and a bargain hunter. And her lips, all slick with pale pink gloss, they look perfect for—

I slam on the brakes. "I don't think it was a street sign."

"It wasn't."

"Not a trash can, either."

"Correct there, too."

I screw up the corner of my lips. "Did you take a tumble down some stairs?"

"Nope."

I snap my fingers. "Sidewalk grate."

Her smile spreads across her face, and that bubbliness is out in full force. "I don't know why I'm smiling. It hurt like the dickens."

"Was it a sidewalk grate left wide open?"

"Do I detect a little fascination with the abomination in your tone?"

I shrug sheepishly. "A little. You can tell me to shut up."

She laughs. "It happened several months ago. I was answering a message from a client, walking down the street like I could handle anything that came my way, click-clacking along, and I smacked into the grate. With my thighs."

"How did you not fall headfirst? I've seen YouTube videos of this happening, and the person almost always falls headfirst."

"Yoga."

I groan inside. Is she one of those yoga-is-life people? Meditation and moon cycles and be-mindfulness bore me to tears. "I always thought yoga was sort of dull. All that *om* would lead to me doing this," I say, then drop my head to the side and snore loudly.

She shoots me a quizzical look, and I realize I've done that thing again—where I say what's on my mind, and I should maybe lock up some of my thoughts more tightly. "Sorry. I meant to say, yoga obviously teaches badass ninja reflexes."

She winks. "Nice save. Although I think it taught me balance, and as soon as I felt I was off-balance, I let myself fall back onto my butt. Maybe you should try yoga since I noticed you might be a candidate for a cell phone mishap, too, someday."

"True, that. But on another note, is there a scar on your butt, too?" My eyes widen, and I cringe. "Shoot. Was that inappropriate?"

"There's no rear-end scar on this booty," she says, smacking her ass, and for a flash of a second, I'm jealous of her palm connecting with her curves.

But that's a strange feeling. Like an errant piece of code. Because why would I want to smack her ass?

"But I did require five stitches on my chin," she adds.

"I never thought I'd meet an in-the-flesh phone-faller," I say.

"And that's why I don't walk and text."

"I completely understand your reticence, and I greatly appreciate you sharing the story of such woe."

"Glad I could entertain you."

I point to Quickie. "Me, too. Should we go into the naughtily named boba tea dealership?"

"Yes, though I should confess I'm not a tea person."

"I'll try not to hold that against you." I yank open the door, then gesture for Evie to step inside.

She smiles appreciatively. "You are a throwback. Such a gentleman."

"What kind of troglodyte wouldn't hold a door for a woman?"

"You'd be surprised at the kind, type, and sheer volume of troglodytes alive and well today." She pauses. "Also, just so you know, most women still appreciate when a man holds the door. So kudos to you. I'm only saying that since I'm sure the future Mrs. Dylan Parker will be grateful."

"Good to know. But she'll probably keep her name, don't you think? I'm not sure she'll want to be Mrs. Dylan Parker."

"Touché. I'm impressed."

"And I'm impressed with this absolutely stunning machine," I say, taking a long look at the white, oval, tea-dispensing contraption parked against the wall.

Glass covers the top half, and inside it, two robotic arms wait to fulfill orders entered via a keypad. A guy with a hat that says Quickie on it is stationed at the counter, next to a sign for fruity tea. He's likely the machine's backup.

"Hey there," I say.

The man narrows his eyes at me. "We kicked your ass last night."

"Come again?"

Evie points to my head. "I suspect he means your Yankees."

I pat my hat. "Oh yeah. Sorry. My sister told me not to wear it." I yank it off, and instantly Evie reaches out a hand and brushes it over the ends of my hair. The gesture startles me but her hand on my hair feels good, too. I blink, trying to figure out why she's touching me.

"Your sister is right. Hair this nice you don't want to hide." Ah, Evie is touching me in her friendly, matchmaker way.

I turn to the dude at the counter, and since he's clearly a Mets fan, I promptly trash-talk the other NY team.

Evie says nothing as we trade zingers at each other, reminding me that she's not into sports. And hey, it's not a requirement that the future Mrs. Parker like sports, but it would sure be fun. After a debate on pitching, the guy gestures to the oval machine. "I should kick you out, but instead I'll let you drink the city's finest boba tea."

I turn to the robotic tea dispenser and meet Evie's eyes. Hers are blue, a shade like tropical waters. I've never noticed them before. Or maybe I've never looked so closely. "What type do I order? I've never tried it."

"I've never tried it, either. Bit of a coffee snob," she says, patting her chest.

"Bit of a tea snob. I should go for jasmine then as the base flavor."

Her eyes light up, even brighter than before. "Ooh, and I should go for black tea, since that's closest to coffee. No sugar—nothing that tastes like a shake."

I shudder. "Neither coffee nor tea should ever taste like a shake."

"Right? We already have milkshakes, and those are awesome enough."

"Milkshakes are unequivocally awesome. We should get milkshakes next time," I say, then I turn from her. Why am I suggesting a next time, as if we're on a date?

I peruse the keypad and input our beverage details. A robotic arm whirs to life. It clunkily stretches and pushes a cup against a spout. Dark liquid fills the plastic cup, then the robot jerks ninety degrees and pushes against a lever. Boba tea balls shoot from a dispenser straw into the cup.

I nearly bounce on my toes as I snap cell phone shots. "It's ridiculously cool."

Evie flashes me a grin. "It is pretty cool."

For a second, I hold her gaze. We might not have much in common, except in this moment we seem to share a bit of hot drink snobbery, as well as an appreciation for this fine machine. As I take the two plastic cups, I remind myself that it doesn't matter what we have in common. She's here to help me find a perfect match.

That's why I refuse to check out her legs as she sits down in the booth.

I take my spot across from her and lift my plastic cup in a toast. "To trying new things," I say.

"I'll drink tea to that."

"Speaking of new things, let's cut to the chase. How does this whole deal work?"

"The one where I find you the love of your life?"

I laugh. "I was thinking the one where you save me from my socially clueless self. But yes, the love of my life works, too."

Chapter Six

Evie

I laugh lightly, loving his ability to poke fun at himself. He's a bit rough around the edges at times, but he also has surprised me with his humor and manners.

Manners have become shockingly overlooked in our society today, but I still contend they go a long way to winning someone's heart.

I wrap a hand around the cup then say, "First, you tell me a little bit about what you're looking for. Be as straightforward as you can because the better I know you, the better I can find somebody who's right for you—who will fall in love with the man. Not the wallet."

He grabs his wallet from his pocket and brandishes it—it's a brown leather billfold. "It's a nice wallet, though. Admit it."

"It's a little small for my taste," I tease.

He leans forward on his elbows. "Don't let the size of the wallet fool you."

"Are you saying what's inside is quite large?"

He wiggles an eyebrow. "I'm saying other things are."

A flush blooms across my cheeks. "Cocky much?"

He gives a carefree shrug. "Maybe I am."

I glance at the table for a moment, because now my mind has traipsed across the dirty meadows to thoughts of large things.

When I look up, I try to affix a thoroughly professional expression on my face. "As I was saying, I know many women in Manhattan. I can vouch for them. I'll only match you with women who are open and interested in the same type of relationship as you are."

"So no flingers need apply?"

"Flinger? That's funny. I haven't heard anyone use that yet. But yes, I'll make sure you're only paired with someone who wants more than a fling." I set down my cup and meet his gaze, making sure he's looking me in the eyes. "It's really heartwarming to meet a guy who knows what he wants and doesn't want to play games."

Now it's his turn to blush, and my stomach surprises me by flipping when I see his cheeks go red. He looks at the straw, his light brown hair flopping over on his forehead. There's something so sweet, almost innocent, about Dylan, but I love his raw honesty and the fact that he seems to know himself so well—flaws and all. So few men, and women for that matter, can hold up a mirror and assess their reflection honestly.

I take my first sip, and holy smokes. This beverage is not supposed to be delicious. I'm supposed to hate it. I suck up three tapioca balls in one strawful, and my eyes widen.

Dylan lifts his drink, and the reaction on his face matches mine as he drinks. "Wow. That was way more fun than it should have been."

"There's something incredibly satisfying about sucking on tapioca balls, I've just learned." I raise an eyebrow naughtily, affording myself this one minor flirtation. "And yes, I do know that sounded dirty."

He holds up his hands in surrender. "I have no problem with dirty."

"You wouldn't. You just made the comment about large things."

"Do you mind large things?"

I roll my eyes. "I have no problem with largesse." I take another drink and bite into a tapioca ball. "This is just so satisfying."

He does the same. "It's sort of like the fork sugar packet game."

"What's that?"

He jumps up from the booth, heads to the counter, and asks for a fork. The Mets fan gives him one, and he returns and grabs a sugar packet from the holder on the table. He positions the packet just so on the end of the fork, then smacks the tines. The pink packet flies up, arcs, and swoops down, landing in my lap.

"Lucky me. I have a sugar packet in my lap."

"Your turn."

I shake my head as I place the packet on the table. "I'm not any good at games."

He arches a brow. "It's a sugar packet. You can do it."

I glance around, like I can find a reasonable excuse to avoid catapulting Sweet'N Lows across a tea shop. But seeing as we're the only customers and Mr. Mets is engrossed in a book, I can't find an out.

"C'mon. You know you want to," Dylan urges. "I'll give you an A+ if you land it in my lap."

"You do know that sounded vaguely dirty, too?"

He wiggles an eyebrow. "I do know." He tips his chin to the fork. "C'mon, Evie. Go wild with me."

From behind his glasses, the green flecks in his eyes seem to dance with mischief. The way he says those words are part-goad, part-flirt, and there's something about him I can't resist. Generally, I try to be poised and polished with clients, but Dylan makes it impossible for me to resist this silly game, plus I know him outside of business. I position the packet on the end of the fork and then drop my hand down. The pink packet shoots high in the air, and I watch as it arcs above us then has the audacity to crash down on my chest.

"Nice boob catch."

"Why thank you. Good thing I had them here for just that reason," I say, taking the sugar packet from my breasts. I hand it to him. "Door prize."

He clutches it to his chest. "I'm keeping this sugar packet forever."

I smile then downshift back to the matter at hand. "So Mrs. Right will be a classy, intelligent, sexy, fun-loving woman who's interested in new experiences and sharing all the good things, from eating out, to movies, to softball, to savoring the adventure of this amazing world together. Tell me more."

He shifts to serious more quickly than I expected. "I like games, as you know. Laser tag. Geocaching. Sports. Anything competitive is my kind of thing," he says, and that reminds me of how different we are. I'm not into sports or competitions. "And it's not like she needs to be on my softball team, but it's just fun to do things together. I want someone with a sense of humor, because at the end of the day, looks fade, but humor lasts."

My heart thumps a little harder. You hardly ever hear that from a man. There's so much focus on looks, but it's deliciously delightful to hear a guy say that's not his top priority. "I absolutely agree with you on that."

"And I want her to be smart since, well, look. I kind of am," he says, looking down briefly, almost as if he's embarrassed.

"Well, you didn't start one of the most successful software

companies without a brain," I point out, since he's well known for founding an augmented reality technology that he and his twin brother then sold for multiple millions to one of the biggest computer giants in the world.

He smiles, and he has such a great smile—full lips and white teeth, and a dimple that lights up the room.

"But mostly, just someone I get along with," Dylan adds with an earnestness that will win many hearts. "I want someone I can go on a long drive with and know we won't run out of things to say. Someone to debate with, and to goof off with. That's what I really want."

"And why now? You're twenty-eight, right?"

"Do you think I'm too young?"

I shake my head, smiling softly. "No, I think people are ready when they're ready."

He taps his chest. "That's me. I've dated. I've had a few somewhat serious girlfriends. But given that I spent so much energy building our company, and now I'm on the other side, I have more time for the social pursuits that weren't a top priority before. But I also think seeing friends like Ryder find that kind of connection made me realize I was ready for my own."

There's something wonderfully beautiful in the simplicity of his answer. "I understand. I see that every day in my walk of life. Sometimes, the lightbulb just goes on, and it's time."

"What about you?"

I shake my head. "Oh no. I'm far too busy and focused on work."

"Ah, got it. So you're *not* looking."

"Nope." I draw a deep drink, sucking down more of the soft, squishy tea balls. "Not looking at all."

He nods several times. "I hear you. You're only ready if you're ready."

"You can't force it. That's why I try to find just the right match for every client." I take another drink of the tea and laugh. "I seriously can't believe I like this. I'm almost ashamed."

He lowers his voice to a whisper. "It's kind of unfairly fun. Like the sugar packet game."

Dylan grabs another packet, and two seconds later, he whacks his fork and sends it right on top of my head.

"Now you're playing dirty," I say, grabbing it from my hair.

I position it on the end of the fork then smack it high in the air, and it lands in Dylan's drink.

He thrusts his arms in the air. "You did it! See? You're a ringer. You're a closet sugar packet fork hockey star and didn't tell me."

"It's one of my many deep, dark secrets."

We chat some more about dates and match-ups, and when we finish our drinks, he clears his throat. "So. Yeah. As you can see, I'm not so well-versed in date protocol. I'm guessing sugar packet fork hockey and talking about tea balls is probably not the best fodder for a first date."

I reach a hand across the table and place it on his forearm. "As I tell my clients, it's best to be yourself. But I still want to meet again and go over some of the things you want, then we can start matching you. What I've found works best is two or three initial consults, so I can really understand what you're looking for. We'll spend more time together and find your perfect match. Would that work?"

His eyes drift down to my hand, and I realize I've lingered too long on him. I yank it back.

"I didn't mind that," he says softly, making me want to say, *I didn't mind, either, especially since your arms are fantastic.*

But I can't flirt with a client any more than I already have. I slide into all-business mode. "And I also want to confirm I'm doing this pro bono."

He makes a clucking sound. "Yeah, about that…"

"Didn't Olivia tell you I offered to do this for free? As a gift to her."

"She did, but I'd rather not be a charity case. I can pay my own way."

I raise my chin. "I'd really like to help. Olivia started as a client and turned into a good friend, and it would truly mean a lot to me to do this free of charge."

"Because I'm hopeless?"

"No! Because you're her brother, and I want to help. Also, to be frank, it's a bit of challenge for me, and I like that. I want to show you that finding a match in person can be better than finding one online."

He raises a skeptical brow. "I still have faith in machines and algorithms. C'mon, don't you know tons of people who met online?"

"Of course. But in some cases, it helps immensely to have a gatekeeper, and I think you saw the proof of that when you ran your ad."

He nods, almost grudgingly, like he can't quite accept the Internet failed him in this case. "But machines are still cool." He waggles the cup of nearly empty tea. "Let's be honest. A robot did make this amazing drink."

I laugh. "Let's make it a game then. Give me a week, and I'll have you on a date with someone I think you can fall in love with."

"Fine. I'll see your offer and raise it. If you introduce me to someone I actually do fall in love with, I'd like to pick up the tab myself."

"And if you wind up back on Plenty of Sharks, obviously it'll remain pro bono and the biggest shame of my professional life," I say with a grin.

He laughs. "Sounds like a deal, and I'll root for you to not wind up on the matchmaking wall of shame," he says, extending a hand to shake. "Want to meet for tacos next time?"

I rein in my disinterest in tacos, reminding myself that tacos aren't a great idea for a date. But of course, he's not taking me on a date. It's a fact-finding mission. "That would be just fine, so long as you know I'm going to advise against taking a woman I match you with to a taco shop. And before we meet, I have some homework for you. I want you to think about your best traits. The top three things you think a woman should know about you."

He makes a T with his hands. "Let's discuss the taco blockade. Do you only represent snobs?"

I roll my eyes. "Dylan, most women don't want to get tacos on a first date."

"Good thing it's not a date then, and good thing I'm not going to take you for anything but the best tacos in the world."

"You're a persistent one."

"I am."

"Fair enough. Take me to the best tacos."

"And I'll think about the three key traits."

"And remember, there's only one rule you should well and truly follow in this real world of dating."

"What's that?"

I fix him with my most serious stare. "Don't sleep together till after the third date."

Chapter Seven

Dylan

This shirt.

Just look at it.

How pretty is this shirt? So pretty you just can't even believe the price tag. I know, I know. I can barely believe it myself. Want to guess how much I plunked down for this royal purple number?

It's six dollars times three.

That's pretty much nothing!

And if you want to find such a deal, let me tell you where to go.

I study the picture of Evie in her purple shirt. At least, I think it's Evie. She doesn't post any photos of her face on her blog. I wonder if it's because she keeps her fashionista blog separate from the matchmaker business, but at the moment, as the train rattles downtown, I'm more interested in the woman behind the shirt than the lesson on how to find a bargain.

Because she looks hot as hell in that shirt. Look at how it clings to her breasts. See how it enhances her natural assets. Admittedly, her breasts are on the smaller side, which is fine by me. I'm not the kind of man who needs to fill his hands—small and perky does the trick for this dude, and Evie looks fantastic in that shirt.

Not that I'm attracted to her. That would be silly. We're polar opposites, and we're in different places. I've been fortunate in that my career skyrocketed before I finished college. I've been on a crazy upward trajectory for the last eight years. Now that my brother and I have sold our company for buckets, I'm working on a passion project—adding some fun new features onto a GPS app that tracks pets. We'll see how it goes, but in the meantime, I wouldn't mind finding someone to share life's moments with.

I wouldn't mind if that someone was pretty, like Evie.

I blink, reminding myself that Evie's job is to find that woman.

I close out her blog, so she can't distract me any longer. As the train rumbles through the tunnels, I answer a few emails, setting a new personal best for speed of response, and hop off the train in SoHo.

I take the steps two by two, heading to meet Evie at the taco shop. I reach the top of the stairs and raise a hand to tug my cap down lower since the sun is casting bolts of sunlight at me. But that's a phantom reaction—Evie gave me marching orders to dress cap-less, and I've followed them.

I squint through my lenses, since I didn't bring my prescription shades. As I stride past a tapas restaurant, I think briefly of Evie's homework assignment. She asked me to focus on the traits that my ideal partner would need to know about me. But she wanted me to push beyond the *I like games, sports, and screens* variety of answers. Will Evie ask me how I would handle different situations? Or my thoughts on politics, religion, and all sorts of ethical debates? Do I need to possess the same philosophical bent as my potential wife?

Wife.

That word reverberates across the gray matter.

I stop in my tracks and stare into a Sur La Table, gazing past the stainless steel pots and fancy pie pans. Am I looking for a wife? Sure, I'm ready for more than casual dating, but I honestly hadn't taken this matchmaking plan to its logical conclusion—a ring on a finger.

I've never wanted to even live with someone. My last girlfriend, Brittany, was fun and sweet, and loved to hike, bike, and skateboard together. But she didn't challenge me enough. I want someone to keep me on my toes. Because that's what I can do for a partner.

I grab my phone and dial my brother, Flynn. He's working in Tokyo this week, pursuing a deal, but with the time difference, he's probably up.

He answers with gravel in his voice. "You better be dead to be calling me now."

"I bit the dust last night. You're talking to me in the afterlife."

He groans. "Seriously. It's six thirty a.m. Why are you calling?"

"Why aren't you up? You're usually out of bed at six a.m."

"There's this thing that happens when you travel to a foreign country. It's called jet lag."

"Right. I figured with yours, you'd be at the fish market now since it opens at six."

"Five, actually. Five twenty-five for the tuna auction, to be precise. And I was there the other day. But even though I've acclimated, on account of being in awesome shape, I decided I'd treat myself to an extra hour of sleep. Anyway, what's up?"

"What three things would you say make me stand out most from other people?"

He clears his throat. "You're a complete pain in the ass. You don't take no for an answer. And you have a ridiculously happy disposition."

I scoff. "Wouldn't point one be at odds with point three?"

"It would if we existed in a perfect theoretical time-space continuum. But we don't. We live in a world with inconsistencies. And that includes you. You're a walking, talking contradiction and a conundrum, as well as an oxymoron, so one and three can coexist perfectly, as they do in you."

I stroke my chin. "Ah, yes. I do enjoy asymmetries living in harmony."

"That's you, little bro. But why do you ask?"

I reach the crosswalk and stop at the red light. "I bit the bullet. I'm going all in with the love pursuit. Olivia sent me to a matchmaker."

"Yeah? That's great," Flynn says, and I fucking love my identical-twin brother for not mocking me this second. Even though we ride each other mercilessly, I'll always have his back, and he'd do the same for me.

"You think so?"

"Absolutely. Just so long as I can put down a bet against the likelihood of you falling in love with someone who can tolerate you."

And I take it all back. I huff. "Have I mentioned you're a complete ass, and I'll be calling you every day, every hour now while you're overseas?"

"No, but have I mentioned I'm not afraid to use the call block feature on my phone?"

"Seriously. Why do you say that about me?" I ask as I cross and turn down the block toward my favorite taqueria.

"Because it's my job to set impossible goals for you."

"It's my job to prove I can exceed them."

"Exactly, man. Exactly. I say it because it'll make you want to prove me wrong. Which is pursuant to my point number two about you. You don't take no for an answer."

"Dammit. You're too smart."

"I am," he says, laughing. "And I'm going back to sleep, since I'm falling in love with my pillow."

"Good night and good morning." I end the call as I near the taco shop, marinating briefly on my brother's assessment. Is he right on all three points, and do those traits serve me or hinder me?

When I reach the shop, I'm surprised to see Evie perched at a counter seat that overlooks the window. She waves broadly at me, and her smile lights up her face. When her grin spreads like that, a charge rushes down my spine, like I've been plugged in.

Like my skin heats up.

It's an unexpected reaction, and I'm not sure what to do with it, so I try to ignore it as I walk inside.

She stands and gives me a hug.

"So we hug," I say, the words coming out stilted because I'm not prepared to be this close to her. *Correction*—I'm not prepared to *like* being this close to her. That electric sensation doesn't abate. It intensifies, crackling through my body and ratcheting up as I catch a whiff of her hair. She smells like a summer breeze, and she fits snugly against my body. Her breasts graze my chest as her arms circle my back.

I count in my head—one, two, three, four—and this embrace officially extends beyond the average socially acceptable time for hugs. But then, what do I know? I've spent so much of my life in the company of screens and machines, of nerds and numbers, and even though I'm no slouch in the ladies' department, I'm not sure if this is the normal time for matchmakers hugging their clients.

"Yes, we hug," she says, repeating my words in the same staccato tone I delivered them in, then pulls back. Her eyes roam up my face, and she raises her brows when she's at hair level. She lifts her hand and ruffles some strands. "See? Why would you ever hide these locks? Your hair is lovely, Dylan."

And that charge skates down my body, pulling on my groin as her hand slides through my hair. "Glad you approve, and I hope you approve of the salsas, too," I say, since it's easier for me to sidestep into my cheap eats mode than to figure out why Evie is making me hard.

Correction: *very hard.*

She gestures to the plate in front of her, filled with a variety of small tubs of salsas. "I was early, so I hope you don't mind that I took the liberty to hand-select some from the salsa bar."

I bring my hand to my chest. "Be still my beating heart. She's punctual, and she likes salsa."

"But I didn't order yet, since I wasn't sure if you wanted to go with just chips, full nachos, or taco-style salsa sampling?"

I decide to test her. "Answer on count of three. One, two, three."

"Nachos," we say in unison, and I raise a hand to high-five her. She smacks back, and I make my way to the counter to order.

I return with a basket covered in cheese, guacamole, and other goodies and sit next to her. "I'll admit it. I'm impressed you already ordered. I didn't peg you for someone who'd embrace the idea of a cheap taco shop, given your taco comment."

She glares at me. "I didn't peg you as someone who'd think I'd limit myself to only the finest dining when out with a client."

"But be honest," I say, as I grab a bean-covered chip. "You're not a frequenter of dirty little taco shops."

She grabs a chip drenched in guacamole and shakes her head. "No. I happen to love upscale sushi best. But I like to think I'm adaptable, and that it's one of my best traits."

I quirk the corner of my lips. "And would another one of your best traits also be lubricating a conversation with a starter comment like that?"

She laughs. "Did you like that segue into the top three traits homework?"

"I did," I say. "Actually, it was quite helpful, because it's a strange thing to have to think about—the three things someone should know about you."

"Did you think about it?" she asks as she scoops her chip into one of the hottest salsas, an orange creamy kind that I fear will burn her tongue off.

I point. "Be careful. The orange is nuclear-hot."

Her blue eyes glint as she bites into the chip without breaking a sweat or fanning the flames in her mouth. She simply chews. Takes a drink of water. And waits for my answer.

"Holy shit," I say as my jaw drops. "Are you an alien? Are you made of steel?"

"Why?"

"You just ate that and didn't react."

"I'm kind of immune to hot things."

"That's insane. Watch this," I say, dipping a chip in the same tub. I bite it, and eat it, but my tongue goes up in flames, and my forehead grows hot with sweat.

"Dylan, have some ice water." She thrusts a cup at me.

I drink it all, then breathe fire. "How did you do that? You're truly not affected by spicy foods?"

"Not the way you are," she says, teasing.

"Oh, that was a low blow."

She leans closer, bumping her shoulder to mine. "Couldn't resist. Forgive me."

My gaze tracks to our shoulders touching, and when her eyes follow, she quickly jerks back. "You're forgiven," I say. "However, I'm going to need to test this superpower with more salsa. Which kind of ties into one of the points you asked me to share. I actually talked to my brother before I saw you and asked him what he thought defined me."

She nods her approval. "Good idea. I suspect he'd know."

I rattle off my traits for Evie—I'm a complete pain in the ass, I won't take no for an answer, and I have a ridiculously happy disposition.

"Which one are you needing to test with me?" she asks.

"It might be that I'm a complete pain in the ass coupled with not taking no for an answer. Do you agree?"

She takes a beat as if she's considering all the sides of the argument, then she nods. "Those seem accurate. But yes, you also seem like a happy person."

"And that's why we should test your superpower. Since it would make me happy."

She laughs. "You're determined to turn this salsa eating into my Achilles' heel."

"I am. That makes me an asshole, doesn't it? Point one."

"I think it just makes you determined, and that's a good trait."

We finish off some more nachos, trying the rest of the salsas, but none attain the level-five lava rating of the orange one, so I grab my phone from my back pocket and search for the closest shop. "Here's the deal. We need cheap tacos, and we need to test your talent."

I hunt for a nearby shop, but before I find one, I remember something. "I better take a photo of this place."

"Why?"

"To post it on Google's search for food reviews. I have more than five million views of my photos of cheap taco shops alongside my ten-word reviews."

Her pretty lips curve up in a curious grin. "You do short and sweet reviews?"

I show her my last one from Captain Habanero in Chelsea. "Good rice, drippy beans, melty cheese equals unsatisfying taco experience."

She points to the black sludge in the photo. "It's like a bean mudslide."

I crack up. "I need to amend my review. Hold on." I hit edit on the text, make some tweaks, then show her. "Good rice can't save bean mudslide lubed with melty cheese."

It's her turn to laugh deeply. "I love it. And you post these for fun?"

I shrug. "I get a kick out of it. It's a hobby." I toggle over to my food app. "Five blocks from here. Let's try Mama June's."

"To Mama June's it is." As we leave, I find my gaze drifting over her body. She wears a royal blue mini-dress that makes her look like she stepped off the set of *Mad Men*, only her dress is shorter than most, the skirt landing right above her knees, showing off her strong, toned legs.

My imagination lingers on her bare legs. "Okay, fess up. Where'd you get those legs?"

She looks down, as if she only just now noticed she has them. "These things?" She waves a hand dismissively. "Ordered them from a catalogue."

"That's impressive, to pick up a pair of legs that excellent from a store. What's the model number?"

"They're called legs, courtesy of walking in Manhattan."

"I thought you were going to say yoga again. Like yoga is the cause of everything."

"Nope. I'm one of those people who is weirdly lucky. I build muscle quickly. I walk everywhere, and it makes my legs strong."

"They're great legs, Evie," I say, since I can't seem to stop admiring them. "And they look good in that cute dress with the floppy collar."

She smooths a hand down the fabric as we continue our quick pace. "Thanks, it's a Peter Pan collar." She fingers the thick white collar. "I snagged it for thirty-three dollars at a shop in Brooklyn."

"I've no idea what a Peter Pan collar is," I say, but I know this—I find her body so damn fetching in it that I want to know what she looks like underneath it. Without it. And that's where my mind travels for the next few seconds.

But that's risky. That's dangerous. My brain is trying to trick me, and I need it on my side. I need it to stop undressing Evie, because she isn't the endgame. She's the means to the end. She's the one who's going to find me the woman I'll love undressing. I try to refocus my thoughts. "By the way, I checked out your blog."

"You did? Are you a closet fashionista?"

"No. I like to research business partners. It was interesting."

She tilts her head curiously. "Why was it interesting?"

I decide to go for broke and tell her, since I just realized what her blog reminds me of.

Chapter Eight

Evie

"It reminds me of me," he says when we reach Mama June's. The dull orange sign is missing a *J. Mama une's.*

"It does?" For some reason this possibility makes me a little giddy.

"I'm kind of ashamed that I only just now connected the dots. But it's not that different. You review fashion and clothes." He taps his sternum. "I review cheap eats."

"Your hobby is my hobby," I say, and that giddy feeling zips through me, like a line of fireflies sparking against the night.

But that's a risky feeling to possess for a client, so I dismiss it immediately. I march to the counter, order chips and salsa this time, and grab a table. The formica is scratched, the napkins fall apart from touching them, and the linoleum floors are badly in need of a scrub. This place is the definition of hole-in-the-wall. It's not my style at all, but Dylan seems to get a kick out of it.

"Do you believe you're a pain in the butt?" I ask, returning to my task of getting to know a client, rather than lingering on a newly realized shared connection.

He takes a chip and dips it into the green salsa, scooping out a dollop. "Probably. But isn't it good to be honest about yourself?"

"I think it is."

"What about you? What if you had to list the traits for a matchmaker that define who you are?"

I tilt my head to the side, considering. "I think I'm an upbeat person. I like to find the positive in nearly everything."

A smile crosses his lips.

"Why are you smiling?"

"You can't steal my answer." He points a finger at me in mock accusation.

My jaw drops. "How am I stealing your answer?"

He taps his chest. "Ridiculously happy disposition."

I pretend to be offended. "You're the only one who's allowed to be cheerful?"

"Yes. I'm claiming good cheer and humor."

I shake my head, narrowing my eyes. "You're not allowed dibs on both, especially since you consider yourself a pain in the ass, too."

"My brother said that. Do you think I'm a PIA?"

I scoop some fiery red salsa and crunch into the chip. It barely registers as mildly hot, while Dylan follows suit and quickly fans his face. When I finish, I dab a napkin on my lips. "I think you're particular, but that's not a bad thing. You seem to know what you like. Whether it's taco shops, tea, robots, tapioca balls, sugar packet hockey, or your work."

"Or finding a woman. Am I particular there, too?"

My answer comes swiftly. "You're not. You're surprisingly not that picky."

He scoffs. "I thought I was."

"It's not a bad thing," I say, reassuring him. "You're open-minded, and that's a bonus when it comes to matters of the heart. You'd be amazed at some of the requests I receive."

"Try me."

"There are men who only want to date models, or women who have C-cup breasts. Others refuse to see anyone who isn't blond, for instance, or older than twenty-eight. That's the biggest line in the sand. So many men have assigned arbitrary age rules."

"Guys are dicks."

"But women are dicks, too," I say, taking another chip. "I have women come to me and say, 'He has to have such and such money' or 'I won't date anyone who makes less than seven figures' or 'Don't set me up with anyone who's under six feet tall'."

"And do you find people for them?"

I laugh and shake my head. "No. I turn them down."

He snaps his head back. "You do?"

"Of course. You didn't take every bit of funding you were offered for your company, did you? If memory serves, you turned down Crossroads Sycamore Capital because you didn't like the terms."

"You researched me?"

"I research all my clients," I say with a smile.

He nods, as if he's impressed. "Sort of like how I researched you earlier. Checking out your blog."

The spark reappears, tripping over my skin, lighting me up. But what a silly reaction. I shouldn't experience hummingbirds in my belly simply because he looked me up. "That's why I don't accept all clients, especially those with unreasonable expectations. I don't think assigning limits is the way to find love or to be happy."

"But I do think it would be great to have reasonable expectations exceeded," he points out.

A smile creeps across my face. I raise a chip in the air. A toast. "To exceeding expectations," I say, tapping my chip against one of his. We dip together, Dylan choosing the salsa verde while I opt for the hotter red salsa. Once he finishes, he takes a drink of water, then gives me an *I'm waiting* look.

"What?" I ask curiously.

"We're not done with you," he says, stabbing his finger against the table. "You've only told me one thing on your list of three."

"You really don't take no for an answer."

He shakes his head. "I don't."

"Fine. Fine." I tap my finger against my lip, noodling on his question. I land on a basic truth about myself. "I can be particular about how I like things done. How I want the bed to be made, the drawers to be closed, the curtains to hang."

His eyes bug out. "You're one of *those* people?"

"First I was a *text-destrian*. Now I'm one of *those* people," I say, rolling my eyes.

"Text-destrian," he says, clearly impressed. "Nice. And yes, you're one of *those* people. A neat freak," he says, as if it's the plague I've caught.

"Neat and owning it. Don't tell me you're a messy slob?"

"No. But I don't understand making beds. I don't get it at all. Just explain it to me. For years, I've wanted to know why it matters. Literally, no one can ever explain the benefit of a made bed. But an unmade bed is genius. You just get back in it at the end of the day. Why make it?"

I draw a deep breath, my mind whirring with images of crisp corners, organized pillows, and carefully aligned comforters. My God, I so love a well-made bed. It brings calm to my soul. "A made bed is beautiful. It signifies neatness. It shows an organized mind."

"Isn't a cluttered mind a good thing? Didn't someone famous say that?"

"Is your computer screen cluttered?" I counter.

He recoils. "No way. I have a neat, clean minimalist desktop."

"And why shouldn't a bed be the same?"

"Because a bed is for sleeping. A computer is for…everything."

The problem solver in me comes out in full force. I must show him the beauty of a made bed. "Come with me." I grab the basket of mostly-eaten chips, dump the rest, return the salsa tubs to the counter for cleaning, and reach into my wallet to leave a generous tip in the jar.

He clasps his hand over mine, shaking his head. "My treat," he says, his voice a soft, sexy whisper. I want to protest, to tell him I insist, but he curls his hand tighter, and I'm speechless.

His hand on mine sparks a wave of goosebumps on my arms, my body telling me I like his hands on me. I want more of his touch. I imagine how I'd feel if he ran his hand up my arm, to my shoulder, through my hair. A shudder races through me, and I do my best to tamp down my reaction to a suddenly overactive imagination.

"Thank you," I say, my voice like a feather.

"You're welcome." His eyes never stray from mine, and for a sliver of time he holds my gaze by the counter at *Mama une's*.

Then I wrestle my attention back to my plan. We leave, and fifteen minutes later, I stroll through the front doors of the Luxe Hotel. My friend Nate Harper is the CEO, and I've texted him for a quick favor. The concierge greets me and hands me a room key card. Dylan and I walk past the chichi sushi restaurant in the lobby, head to the elevator, and soon arrive at room 521. I slide the card in the door.

Dylan sets a hand on my arm. "Are you trying to seduce me?"

"No," I say quickly. Too quickly. I'm not trying to seduce him at all.

I open the door, and a perfectly modulated blast of cool air greets us. We stroll across the navy carpet to a king-size bed perfectly appointed with a gorgeous white duvet and mountains of blue velvet pillows. I gesture to it, as if I'm a saleswoman, showing it off. "Tell me. Doesn't this bed make you want to do everything on it?"

Then, to demonstrate my point, I fall back onto it, like a snow angel.

I prop myself on my elbows and meet his eyes. His green irises darken, and his lips part. He stares at me, and something shifts. The look in his eyes is no longer challenging. He's not asking me to prove a point. His eyes are hungry. He stares as if he's considering my question seriously, and I realize that maybe it does sound as if I'm trying to seduce him. I've pushed the limits here. I'm in a hotel room, trying to prove a point to a client, and in reality, my skirt is riding up my thighs, and I'm sprawled on a pristine, inviting bed.

This kind of bed is designed not only for sleeping, but for the best kind of sex in the world—hotel sex. The kind of loud, dirty, wild sex you can have when you don't have to make the bed in the morning.

For a flash, I see Dylan hovering over me. Pinning my wrists. Pressing his body against mine. A wave of heat washes over me, and my skin is flush, my heart slamming hard against my chest.

I want that.

I want to feel that abandon.

And that goes against my personal code of ethics as a matchmaker—*thou shalt not fall for a client.*

I glance down, and see my skirt is riding up. It hits mid-thigh, revealing more of my legs. I tug it, and when I look up, Dylan is staring at me with darkened eyes. "Yeah. This bed makes me want to do everything on it."

* * * *

In the elevator, I speak first. "The third thing is sometimes I push to make a point."

"Do you?" He gazes at me as the elevator chugs downward.

I nod, swallowing. My throat is dry. "I do. I just did."

His lips quirk up. "I think I like that side of you."

I like a lot of sides of him, and that's becoming a problem.

Chapter Nine

Dylan

I round the corner in Gotham and fire off a ray of light at an ad technology dude in jeans and a black hoodie. It lands right in the middle of his spine. I double back and ambush a redheaded woman who runs a business consulting firm. She curses admirably and crumples dramatically. I deliver a punishing shot to a short, bearded guy who peddles enterprise software, and I'm nine for ten.

When the game ends, my breath comes fast from the running, and Mia shakes her head in admiration.

"You're on fire today," she says as we make our way out to turn in our weapons. "Glad I'm in town when you're playing at the top of your game."

I grumble something about needing the release.

"Sorry. Can't hear you over your annoyed mood."

"I'm not annoyed. Just…"

"Just what? Are you irked over the whole dating thing?"

"No. It's just that…"

"Tell your friend Mia," she says encouragingly.

"Why don't you tell me about Patrick?"

She shakes her head. "How many times do I have to tell you there's nothing to tell?"

"Really?"

"We're only friends. That's all." She slashes a hand through the air to emphasize how *only* friends she is.

"I doubt it."

"Anyway, how is our lovely matchmaker? Is Patrick's sister finding you a fabulous lady to love?"

"She's working on it," I say, but the thing is, I like spending time with Evie more than I should. More than I expected to. But I'm not sure if I should say that to Mia. In fact, I should probably keep my lips zipped. Evie and I aren't in the cards. She's not interested in a relationship, and I'm not interested in a crush that goes nowhere.

It's best to reboot to business—the business of finding love.

"It's going great," I say, with my ridiculously happy disposition.

"She's fun, isn't she? Sharp, too. I like her," Mia says, drumming her fingers against the counter as I turn in the weapons.

"Yeah. Me, too."

Interlude

Sometimes, the story reaches a fork in the road. Our hero can go one way, our fair heroine another. What's a storyteller to do when such a happenstance occurs? Every now and then, in the middle of a tale, someone needs a nudge. A wink. Maybe even a shove. After all, even when two people seem like a fit to others, they often still can't see what's in front of their noses. One needs to hold up a mirror for them.

Chapter Ten

Evie

There is dirt. There are trees. There are bushes, and bugs, and creepy crawlies.

I can't believe I'm hiking.

"Am I going to be attacked by a snake?" I ask Patrick as I scan behind me for slithery creatures.

"Nope," he says, marching confidently forward. "Just bears."

I jump. "Where?"

He points in the distance, beyond the bend in this trail rolling along the Hudson River shorefront, one of my brother's regular haunts for his adventure tour business.

"Are you kidding?" I ask, my voice squeaking.

My big, tall, burly brother laughs, tossing his head back as he stops in his tracks. "You're such a city girl."

I park my hands on my hips and stare sternly down my nose. Or up my nose, since Patrick is ten feet taller than me. But, in defense of my height, he's ten feet taller than most people.

"Are. There. Bears?"

He rolls his eyes and gestures to the cliffs overlooking the river, and the sweeping views of Manhattan in the distance. "No bears. But check out the bird of prey." He points above to a toweringly tall tree.

I follow his hand to a high branch, claimed by a hawk.

"Birds of prey know they're cool," I say, reciting a favorite cartoon line, and Patrick raises a fist to bump with mine. We used to read *The*

Far Side together when we were kids. Patrick and I actually get along well for siblings, even though we're opposites in many ways—I'm a city girl, and he's the king of the outdoors. But he has a soft heart and a witty brain, and we've both sparred and played well over the years.

"Also, would I ever put you in harm's way?"

"You better not," I say, and we resume our pace.

"I like you too much to let a bear get you."

"Aww, you're sweet," I say as we crunch along the trail, Patrick several paces ahead.

A tree branch rustles in the breeze and the water gurgles. "Besides, if a bear shows up, all I have to do is outrun you," he deadpans.

I lunge at him, jumping on his back, crawling up him like a lemur, and delivering an absolutely punishing noogie. "You're dead to me," I mutter.

Patrick cracks up.

As I jump off him, I say, "I'm going to tell Mia you use women as bear shields."

He turns around and gives me a *huh* look. "Why would you tell Mia?"

"Because you're into her?" I ask, suddenly confused.

He arches a brow. "I am?"

Make that even more confused. "I thought you two were a thing. I saw you chatting with her at the dinner party at Max and Henley's a few weeks ago. Isn't there something there?"

He winks and slugs my arm. "Just kidding. I have it bad for Mia, but I'm not sure I'm her type."

I move my arms jerkily and speak in a robotic voice. "Does. Not. Compute. Woman who does not fall for Patrick's charms."

"Ha ha," he says as the hawk sails overhead, scouring the skies. "Some women are strangely immune to me." He clears his throat. "But, um, what about you? And that guy?"

"What guy? I'm not seeing anyone."

"I thought you were helping someone," he says, and the words come out awkward, which in itself is odd since Patrick and I usually chat comfortably about dating.

"You mean my new client?"

He snaps his fingers as he stops to gaze at the water and the picnic-perfect views. "That's it. The Stud Finder is finding a studette. Any luck?"

For a brief moment, I wonder if Patrick is asking if I'm into Dylan. I don't want to let on, though, so I keep my answer all business. "Not yet, but I'm still getting to know him so I can make the right match."

He clears his throat. "And do you dig him?"

I tilt my head to the side, studying his face. "Why would I dig him? He's a client."

Patrick drags a hand through his light brown hair, the look on his face flustered. It's a look I don't see him wear often. "I thought you and Dylan had a connection," he says, in that flummoxed tone again.

I furrow my brow. "Why would you think that?"

"I don't know," he says, tossing up his hands. "But the way you deny it makes me wonder."

I part my lips to practice denial once more, but I think better of it. I go for truth, because I need to say it. "If you must know, I actually think he's quite handsome and way more fun than I ever expected, and we have more in common than I imagined…but…"

"There's always a but."

"But he's a client, Patrick," I say, a note of desperation threading through my voice. "It would be wrong to fall for him."

"Can't mess around with the customers," he says, nodding, since that's one of his golden rules, too.

"Exactly."

He tips his forehead to the hawk, circling high above. "That hawk would break the rules, though."

"That's why he's a hawk. He can do whatever he wants."

For the first time ever, I kind of want to be a hawk.

Chapter Eleven

Dylan

The banging on the door can only mean my sister is here. Nobody else can bang that loudly.

Pound. Pound. Pound.

I stride across the hardwood floors and unlock the door to my loft apartment. "How does one person pack so much punch into her fist?"

"I'm mighty," she shouts as she marches in.

"And you're *here*." I point to the floor since I wasn't expecting her.

"Of course I'm here. Because of your text." She waves her phone at me, as if it's been naughty. "Seriously? You don't know what to wear to yoga?"

I heave a sigh. "I sent you a text message. You don't need to arrive like the cavalry."

"Oh, I do. I very much do." She marches past me into my bedroom.

"Hello? Bedroom. Respect privacy much?"

Her eyes shoot laser beams at me. "Is that a real question? My whole career is predicated on both respecting and disrespecting privacy."

"True."

She reaches my bureau and parks her hands on her hips. "All right. Let's do this."

"Olivia, all I want to know is if I have to get a pair of fucking yoga pants."

She shakes her head. "I can't take a chance of you messing this up.

If you think you're wearing yoga pants to a yoga class, I know you'll show up dressed like Richard Simmons, like the time you wore too short shorts to a roller-skating party."

"Do you really have to remind me of that?" I cringe, remembering the height of my dorkitude in middle school, when I was invited to a party at the roller rink and showed up in an outfit that should have been banned a decade prior. In my defense, there was nothing in HTML or C++ code about the proper attire for a roller-skating party, and I'd had my face in front of a screen when I was twelve.

And when I was sixteen. And twenty, and so on.

"I do. I do have to remind you of that," Olivia says as she loops her brown hair into a bun. "Because you can't go to yoga wearing yoga pants. Cool guys don't wear yoga pants to yoga class."

"No worries there since I'm not cool."

"You're cool enough."

"What do I wear then?"

"Basketball shorts and a gray T-shirt."

"That's weirdly specific."

She looks to the window, speaking softly. "It's what Herb wears when he goes to spin classes."

"Herb does spin classes?" I ask as I open the drawer containing my gym shorts.

She snaps her gaze back to me. "He does, and he looks hot."

I wiggle my eyebrows. "You want me to look hot like your soon-to-be husband?"

She grabs a pair of shorts from the open drawer and launches them at me, like a missile. I grab them before they flutter to the floor.

"No. I just want to save you from yourself."

"So noble. And all you had to do was text me to tell me to wear basketball shorts and a T-shirt."

"I know, but even by text you'd think it meant something else."

"Duly noted. But, um, why not yoga pants or yoga shorts?" I ask, curiosity getting the better of me.

She makes a noise with her throat. It grows louder and louder. "Because if anything gets, you know…" Her eyes drift downward.

"YOU MEAN IF I GET A BONER?"

Her face flushes beet red. "Don't say that ever again."

"You brought it up."

"Also, why are you going to yoga with Evie? You hate yoga."

There it is—the million-dollar question. I'm going to yoga because I know I'll hate it. I'm going to yoga because I can't risk going near a hotel room or out to dinner with a woman I'm trying my damnedest to be unattracted to. Yoga is a recipe for killing this bizarre and unexpected lust I feel for my matchmaker.

"Evie wants to discuss what worked well and didn't work well on some of my recent dates before I started working with her, so I suggested we do yoga and talk after."

"I can't picture you doing yoga."

"Good. Let's keep it that way."

Since I have no intention of doing yoga ever again.

* * * *

Yoga pants.

Damn it.

Why didn't I think about how absolutely fucking delicious she'd look in yoga pants? I was so fixated on not wearing hot pants that I never thought about how hot she'd look in hers.

The fabric hugs her ass.

The material worships her legs.

The cotton caresses her calves.

I nearly whimper at her downward dog in front of me.

I am a dog as I stare at her ass.

"That's right. *Feel* your palms dig into the mat, and push your feet as flat as you can against the floor," the teacher says, her calm voice wafting across the yoga studio, making me want to roll my eyes. "Feel all your energy drive into your feet, and then flow back through your body."

It's all such mumbo jumbo, but nonetheless, the straight A student in me is programmed to listen to teachers, since school was the boxing ring where I dominated. I adjust my stance, picturing my feet pressing against the floor like anchors, as she instructs.

"Good. Now, hold that stance with your hips driving down," the curly-haired teacher intones.

I'd like to drive into the woman in front of me.

And I wobble. I fucking wobble to the side, the floor tilting precariously closer. And then, yep. The floor hits me. Damn floor. My shoulder lands first with a loud *thwack.*

Evie pops up. "Are you okay?"

I shake it off, getting back into position. "Yep. Just fine."

The teacher floats over, and I wave her off. "I'm all good."

"Are you sure?"

"Everything is fine," I say, with the confidence that helped me pull off the multimillion-dollar sale of our company. I might have a dork still in me, but I know how to go full business stud when I have to.

Like when I fall on my fucking shoulder.

Besides, everything is fine since at least now I'm not aroused in class anymore.

A little later, we turn ninety degrees as the teacher begins a series of tree poses, and I try to keep my focus ahead of me, but out of the corner of my eye, I watch Evie, now to my side.

She digs her left heel into the ground and slides her right foot up her inner left leg.

"That's right." The teacher nods at Evie, who's fashioning herself into a flamingo.

"Everyone can reach a different place here," the teacher says. "Some might keep your right foot mostly on the floor. Others might rest against the ankle, others the calf, and others the knee. It's not a contest. It's a mindset."

I refrain from rolling my eyes, even as I only manage to position the bottom of my foot against my ankle.

But Pretzel Girl? Evie hikes that leg up high, so damn high, she plants her foot against her upper inner thigh.

The teacher strides across the room. "The focus is balance. Look straight ahead and balance."

Evie stares intensely at the wall as she stands on one leg. Her body is tight, her concentration stellar, and she wriggles her right foot higher, and higher still, as if she's waging war to claim the Most Flexible Body in the Class prize.

The teacher walks past her, then stops, doubles back and sets her hands on Evie's hips, wiggling her. "Move your foot lower."

"But I can keep it here," Evie says tightly.

A smile crosses the teacher's placid face. "I'm sure you can, but it's not a competition. The goal is balance, not maximum flexibility."

The teacher nudges Evie's foot lower, to her knee. Evie huffs when the teacher walks away. Then she looks at me and sticks out her tongue at the teacher.

My eyes widen, and holy shit.
I think I might really like her.
A lot.

* * * *

"You're a closet yoga competitor," I whisper as we leave the studio and head toward Central Park.

Evie flutters her lashes innocently. "Who said I was competing?"

I nudge her shoulder.

"Who, me?" she asks, feigning innocence.

Something bubbles inside me. A feeling of excitement. Of desire. Or true and honest *like*.

"You were one hundred percent practicing competitive yoga."

We stride toward the park. "Fine," she says, spitting it out like it costs her something. "I was. It's my dirty little secret." She stops and turns to me, words spilling out of her like a confessional. "I go to yoga, and it's slow. I make it a game. In my head, I pretend I'm competing for the most flexible award. And since I'm terrible at sports, this is the one area I'm weirdly good at. So I pretend to compete, and it drives me crazy when the teacher calls me on it. Like, why can't I pretend to compete in a flexibility game?" She digs her hands into her hair. "I feel terrible saying this."

"Welcome to the competitive club. We have jackets."

She lets out a long breath. "Oh God, it feels so good to admit this though. I love yoga and do it because it's good for me, but sometimes it's slow, so I make it more fun, like a game," she says, grabbing my shoulders to emphasize her point.

Yeah, she can grab my shoulders anytime. And by anytime, I mean she can pull me closer. Bring me deeper, wrap her arms around me.

What the hell? I'm doing it again. Fantasizing. But then, she's the one staring at me, with her hands curled over my shoulders.

"I'm also like that," I say. The street sign ticks behind us, indicating the light has changed.

"I know. When does it stop? The crazy competitive drive." She lets go of me, and we cross the street.

"I don't think it ever does," I say, snagging a bench inside the park. "You'll probably become one of those people at the gym who pretends to race on the exercise bike against the woman next to her."

She clasps her hand to her mouth. "Oh God, I've done that."

My lips quirk up. "Maybe you even take the stairs at the airport instead of the escalator, and see if you can make it up faster while carrying a suitcase."

Her eyes widen. "Guilty as charged."

I lean in closer, going for the zinger. "I bet you even do it on moving walkways. You'll see if you can walk faster than the people on the motorized one."

She grabs her cheeks, her expression turning to *The Scream.*

"Don't be ashamed. Just accept that you're truly a competitive beast."

Nodding, she settles, taking a breath. "I am Evie, competitive beast."

I pump a fist. "Knew I could get you to admit it. Also, takes one to know one."

"And to think, I'm supposed to be getting to know you better, and here you are, reading me like an open book."

"Hey, you aren't an open book. Not every Tom, Dick, or Harry could add up the clues about you. I paid attention," I say, meeting her blue-eyed gaze.

Her expression goes softer. Her eyes sparkle, and her lips curve into a gentle smile. Her eyes stay locked with mine, and the silence feels important. Like it could lead to something. "You do pay attention. I like that."

And I like so many things about her.

Like the way she looks at me. How the tip of her tongue darts out to lick her lip. How her eyes don't stray from mine. Most of all, how my body seems to hum when she's near me, and I'm dying to know if she feels the same.

She squares her shoulders. "But I need to get to know a few more details so I can set you up on your dates. Did you do your homework? Can you tell me what you liked and didn't like in your last few dates?"

And here we are again.

It's not the same for her.

But she sounds more serious than I've heard her speak before. More professional. Like she's trying to be a pro.

"I went to a beer festival with a woman on the laser tag team. She was easygoing, which I like. But she kept taking selfies the whole time, which I didn't like."

"I don't think I'd like that, either."

"A few months ago, I played mini golf with a venture capitalist I met at a happy-hour shindig. She spent most of the time talking about herself. Not a fan of that."

"Nor am I."

"And then I went to the movies with another woman, and she slept through half the flick."

Evie laughs. "She must have been quite tired."

"In her defense, she did a movie recap with me after the closing credits, and that was weirdly fun to hear her review a movie she'd half seen."

"Duly noted—weird fun can be good."

That's all I say about other dates. What I want is to know Evie even better. Since the more I learn, the more I realize we're actually a lot alike.

She tells me about the women she has in mind for me, rattling each one off on a finger. An athletic woman who runs her own advertising agency and has season tickets to the Yankees, a photographer who's also a foodie and loves to sample the goods at food trucks, and a pretty chemist who is a poker player.

The women all sound great. I bet they're fantastic ladies.

But I don't want to date them.

What I want to do is convince Evie to date me. That's my new goal, so I toss her question back at her. "Tell me about your last dates."

Chapter Twelve

Evie

"I can't even remember when my last date was," I tell him.

He narrows his eyes. "Yes, you can."

"It was months ago. I really can't remember."

"For real?"

I cross my heart. "I've been so consumed with work, I truly haven't had time."

The look he gives me is skeptical. "With all the men in your Rolodex, you've never been tempted to date one?"

Dylan stretches his arm behind us on the bench. I half wish I was seventeen again, and this was the pre-make-out-during-the-movies move. But he's simply stretching, and I'm simply wishing for a *more* that can't happen.

I shake my head. "No, it's not my place to dip into the Rolodex."

He bangs his palm against the slats of the bench. "And you never wanted to?"

Not till now. Not at all.

"Nope," I say, punctuating the *P* to emphasize how un-tempted I am.

He nods several times, as if he's letting the thought soak in. Then he cocks his head to the side, his eyes challenging me. "Does that mean the men in your Rolodex are duds?"

"No! Of course not," I say, indignant. "They're fantastic, intelligent, kind, handsome—"

I stop, realizing I walked right into that.

He laughs. "Then, how have you never been tempted?"

"You set me up," I say, smacking his thigh.

"Sure, but I want your response." He shifts closer to me. "Remember, I don't take no for an answer. Tell me the truth."

I draw a breath. "I've never been tempted because I can't let myself be tempted. It would compromise my integrity. I need to make sure my clients trust me completely."

"But they do, Evie."

Something about the way he says my name sends a charge through me. A hot spark settles between my legs, like a quiet pulse.

Out of the corner of my eye, I see his fingers inching closer to my shoulder, almost as if he's tempted to touch me. I want him to. So badly. I want those fingers to slide over my shoulders. To brush along the curve of my neck. To thread through my hair.

What am I doing?

Dylan is my client's brother.

Dylan is now my client.

I'm not interested in a match for myself. I'm not looking for love. I'm focused on work, and Dylan is my work.

The trouble is, my work turns me on more than I expected, and that's for one elemental reason—I like him.

I like him so very much.

That's why I jerk this conversation back to the purpose of these get-togethers—prepping him for his princess charming, whoever she may be.

I brush one palm against the other. "The big question is—are you ready for me to set you up on your first date? Or do you think the fall in yoga has set you back?" I wink.

"You think falling in yoga means I'm not ready to date?"

I laugh. Nervously. "Well, not entirely. But it did remind me what we talked about before we had tea. That we all have a bit of dork in us. So, I didn't know if you wanted to walk through all the potential topics, moments, pitfalls, and so on."

"Like a pre-date prep? Or maybe even a practice session?"

"Sure, we can practice now if you'd like," I offer.

He doesn't answer right away. When he does, he takes his time, like he's making an offer. "Or maybe we can practice in a true date simulation."

Tingles race over my shoulders. "Like a practice date?"

His eyes twinkle like stars. "I need a practice date badly. Can I take you on one? It would be so helpful to review everything. Make sure I'm ready."

When he puts it like that... "Yes, of course."

I want him to put his best foot forward. I didn't say yes because I want to date him. I wouldn't do that, even though when he walks away, all I can think is how on earth did I wind up with a pitter-pattering heart for a man I'm handing off to another woman?

* * * *

"So?"

Olivia blows on the sky blue polish on her fingernails. She's perched across from me at the salon, an expectant look on her face.

"A needle pulling thread?" I counter.

"So...how's it going with my brother?" she asks as the nail technician spreads the bristles in the brush against my big toe.

"It's great!" I say in my best chipper, cheery, Matchy-McMatcherson voice. We've been chatting about her wedding plans for most of the mani-pedi, and I'd been meaning to give myself a pat on the back for successfully steering the conversation away from thoughts of how much I want to get naked with her brother.

But I don't only want to roll in the hay with him.

If that was all I wanted, I'd simply flash his image in the movie screen of my mind and take him for a few solo trips at night to get him out of my system.

It's more than that. I haven't wanted to date anyone in a long, long time. Now, I want to date him. I want him to choose me. To tell me I'm the one he wants to share jokes with, try new things with, visit hole-in-the-wall Mexican joints with.

But there's another reason why dating Dylan would be risky. I'm looking at that reason. Olivia's a client who's become a friend. She came to me with a request—to help her brother. Not to bed her brother. I can't try to claim him for myself when my job is to unearth the best woman for him.

"And when will his first big date be?"

"I'm thinking one more week," I say, my newly polished peach fingernails curling over the arms of the chair, gripping it.

One more week till another woman can have a chance at this fun, clever, kind, sometimes pushy, occasionally pig-headed but always big-hearted man.

"The clock is ticking until his first big date," Olivia says, moving her fingers back and forth like a pendulum, reminding me that time is winding down. And with that knowledge in mind, that this is the last time I'll see Dylan one-on-one, the last time I'll have his presence all to myself, I decide to make the most of my practice date.

Later that night, I shower, curl the ends of my hair, spritz on my favorite scent, and slip into a pretty, pale blue shift dress that hits just above my knees.

I slide on a pair of silvery sandals that lift me two inches higher. It doesn't escape my attention that they make my legs look strong, and that Dylan likes my legs.

I fasten my necklace with a tiny matchbox pendant, Patrick's gift to me when I started my business.

And when I leave to head to the sushi restaurant he suggested, I repeat my mantra over and over.

It's not a real date, it's not a real date, it's not a real date.

But when I reach the restaurant in the lobby of the Luxe, and he's waiting for me at the bar, a dark blue button-down rolled up, showing off his forearms, his smile as adorable as ever and those eyes glinting from behind his glasses, I fear I might need a new mantra.

Because this feels exactly like a date.

Chapter Thirteen

Dylan

She looks like a naughty princess.

Wait.

She only looks naughty because I'm thinking of her naked.

So, that's on me.

I rise, walk over to her, and press a kiss to her cheek. A faint whoosh of breath seems to rush from her lips, and that sound knocks a few filters loose in my brain. Before I know it, I blurt out, "You look like a dirty angel."

Then I wrench back, instantly regretting the words.

"What did you say?" she asks, a smile playing on her lips.

"You look like an angel," I offer, selling it with the kind of confidence I rely on when pitching venture capitalists.

It seems to work, since Evie smiles and runs her fingers briefly over my collar. "You look quite handsome," she says, then pats my chest. "Perfect first-date wear."

"It was a toss-up between this and overalls. Glad you like the one I picked."

"Overalls then for date two," she says with a wink.

The hostess appears at our side and asks if we're ready to be seated.

"Absolutely," I tell her, and we follow the woman in the black dress to a quiet booth near the back of the restaurant. Three votive candles in short tin cups form a circle, their lights flickering in the darkened corner.

Evie sits first, and when I take my seat, the hostess hands us menus.

As I peruse mine, a strange spate of nerves crawls up my throat. But I dismiss them. There are nerves and there are decisions. I've made mine, and I know what I want.

Her.

Soon, the server comes to our table and introduces himself as Oliver. We order sake, edamame, and I add in a seaweed salad. Evie arches a brow and mouths *seaweed?* She points to her teeth and slides her fingers along them.

"Cancel the seaweed salad, please," I tell the stocky man. "What would you recommend instead for an appetizer, Oliver?"

"Do you like scallops? We have a seared scallop appetizer that melts in your mouth."

I look to Evie, letting her answer.

"Love them," she says.

"Me, too. We'll have the seared scallops instead."

"And what would you like from the sushi menu?"

Evie chooses a rainbow roll and unagi, and I opt for yellowtail and mackerel.

"Excellent choices," the waiter says with a nod. "And if there's anything else I can get for you, don't hesitate to let me know."

"We definitely will. Thanks, Oliver."

The waiter leaves, and Evie is grinning at me.

"What?" I bare my teeth. "Do I already have seaweed stuck in my teeth, and I didn't even order it?"

She shakes her head, her smile never vacating her pretty face. "They say on a first date, you can tell more about a man from how he treats the waiter than anything else."

"And what did you learn?"

"You were quite nice to him."

"Why would anyone not be nice, though? I don't get it. I don't get why someone would treat a waiter, a server, a cabbie, a hotel clerk, a salesperson—anyone—like a douche."

"I don't know, either, but it happens."

"I don't need to put someone down to feel good about myself."

She rests her chin in her hand, studying my face. "You're an interesting man, Dylan."

"Am I?" I peer at her over the top of my glasses.

"You are. So tell me, what do you do for a living?" She rolls her hands, saying *go with it.*

"Oh, is this the role-play?"

She nods. "Practice date banter."

I chuckle, mostly to myself, since it seems too silly to put the car in reverse. But I have to remind myself that Evie is on the clock and doing her job. "I'm an entrepreneur."

Her blue eyes sparkle. "How interesting. Do you love it?"

"Absolutely. I've wanted to start my own company since I was a kid, and I love making things, growing a business, building it up, and selling it for gobs of money. What about you?"

"I'm a matchmaker, and yes, I always wanted to do this."

"How so?"

"When I was a little girl, I loved setting up my dolls."

I crack up, enjoying the image of her playing matchmaker to dolls. "Seriously?"

"I had a purple bucket of Ken and Barbie dolls as well as a stuffed panda, and the panda served as the great arbiter of romance amongst the dolls, deciding which couple would be allowed to spend a night in the Barbie house."

I drag a hand through my hair. "That might be one of the best stories ever. Since basically, you are now the stuffed panda."

She laughs, leaning forward, a few strands of her blond hair framing her face. "I was. I also loved to match clothes and colors, and I think over time, all the skills and interests coalesced."

The waiter returns with the drinks and appetizers, and we both thank him, then dive into the scallops.

As I lift the chopsticks, I ask, "And do you love what you do?"

She chews then answers. "I do. It's honestly one of the most fulfilling things I can imagine doing. I'm very fortunate in that I've made several quite successful matches, and I have some incredibly satisfied clients. They're happy, they're in love, they want to be together for the rest of their lives. I can't ask for anything more."

"Makes you feel lucky, right? Blessed even?" I ask as I pop an edamame into my mouth. "To do what you love, to be successful at it, to know it matters to others."

"Yes, that's exactly how I feel."

She lifts her sake cup and drinks, and I watch her. From the hair to the dress to the lip gloss, Evie is so well appointed, put together. She's polished, and I bet she's been called pretty her whole life because the whole package comes together. But to me, she's sexy and sensual.

Because I'm turned on by her mind, by her mouth, by her outlook. The combination is what makes a woman sexy.

She blinks, as if she's coming to after slipping into another plane of reality. "I just realized I'm not doing a very good job helping you practice for a date."

"Why do you say that?"

"We're sitting here talking about me, not prepping you."

"But I'm having fun."

"Are you?"

I hold up my palm, taking an oath on an imaginary Bible in court. "I swear."

A faint smile crosses her lips. "You seem very comfortable. More so than the first time we met, and definitely more than at yoga."

I pretend to blow on my fingernails. "Guess you made a swan of this ugly duckling."

She scoffs. "You're not ugly. You're not a duckling, and there was no *Pygmalion* transformation here. Just a few little bits of encouragement."

"Not ugly?" I sketch air quotes. "That's my biggest goal in life. To be *not ugly*."

She tosses her napkin at me. "Oh, stop it. You know you're handsome."

And I like that compliment a helluva lot. "Am I?"

"Incredibly handsome."

Pride surges through me, alongside a fresh dose of confidence.

Until she says the next thing.

She pats my hand. "You're going to make some woman quite happy."

But not her.

My heart smashes to the floor.

Chapter Fourteen

Evie

A piece of eel sits atop the rice between the ends of the two orange chopsticks. "This sushi is amazing."

"Yeah, it's great." Dylan smiles, but it doesn't reach his eyes.

His response only makes me amp up my sales pitch. "I love unagi." I bring the slice to my mouth and devour it, rolling my eyes in pleasure. "So good," I declare when I finish.

"Yeah, I knew you liked sushi." His tone is flat.

The mood has shifted. The easy, breezy atmosphere has been zipped up and sealed away in a plastic bag. In its place, Dylan is a perfectly suitable date—polite and considerate. But that's all.

I keep trying. Broadening my smile. Rocketing up the conversation. Adding even more pom-poms. "I'm so glad we came here. It's such a great idea to try new restaurants."

"Yeah."

I'm a used car salesman. I can't let go. "Where else do you think you'd want to go on a date?"

His brow knits. "Excuse me?"

I take a drink of my sake and set down the china cup. "Well, I'm thinking about the series Ryder did—ten dates to falling in love. Do you know that?"

"I'm aware of his work."

"I want to set you up for a successful experience. Do you want to geocache, go to the arcade, see a basketball game?" I ask, but I don't wait for his answer. I can't blurt out that I have feelings for him and ruin our business relationship, so I need to salvage this evening. All I can think is to layer on a good mood, a better mood, the best mood. "Oh, that's it, I bet. Probably a basketball game. Maybe with the woman who has the season tickets? I bet she'd love that." I fish around in my purse for a small notebook. "I'm just going to jot this down."

"Evie." His voice is heavy. It says *stop*.

But if I stop I'll have to face the fact that I have feelings for him.

"It's a good idea, though. Don't you think?" Brightness defines my face right now. So much brightness, it will overwhelm all the weirdness.

He scrubs a hand over his jaw, then he sighs. "Whatever you decide for a date is fine." He clears his throat, spreads his hands on the table, and leans closer. His eyes lock with mine, and my breath escapes my chest. For a split second, he glances at the ceiling and shakes his head, then he seems ready. "All I want is to find someone I connect with. The setting doesn't matter. Hell, we could get cheap tacos, sit on a park bench, or sample salsa, and it would be fine."

He lets his gaze linger on mine longer than I expect, and his words feel important. As if he's trying to tell me something beyond what's been spoken. My stomach flips, and tingles launch an all-out butterfly assault on my body. Is he saying he's liked these un-dates? That he feels the same connection? And what the hell do I do about it? Do I report myself to the international matchmaker consortium for committing the unspeakable violation of falling for a client?

Fine, fine. It's not technically a violation. Only I can't help but think I've been dipping into the kitty and skimming off the top. Even if he likes spending time with me, that doesn't mean I should ask him to date me, only me.

Or does it?

Choose me, I want to say.

I want to sweep my hand across the table of all the other women and knock them to the ground like spilled dishes.

This possessiveness is wholly new to me.

Another thing is, too.

A desire to make more time for him.

To carve out another hour here, another hour there. To make him a priority. I haven't felt this way for anyone in ages, and I don't know what to do next. Since he seems to be speaking from the heart, I follow his lead. "Or those delicious tapioca tea balls that you never thought you'd like."

The corner of his lips twitch. "It's good to experience new things, don't you think?"

Heat flows through me, unfurling and warming me everywhere. "I like experiencing new things," I say and my voice sounds breathless to my own ears.

I wonder how it must sound to him. If he can tell I'm burning up across from him. I cast my gaze to the exit, my mind leaping ahead. Then I look back at Dylan, where his eyes are dark, even behind his lenses.

I draw a breath, and my lips part. They're an invitation, and he has to know. He has to be able to tell I'm ready to launch myself at him.

He reads my body language. He stands up, moves to my side, and slides next to me, brushing a strand of hair over my ear. I shudder. He dips his face near mine. "I'd really like to kiss you right now."

All the tension, all the hoping, unspools. All I can do is whisper *yes* to him.

His lips are on mine, and I melt into the sweetest kiss. It's soft, but confident. It says he'll take his time, that he wants this. He wants me. He slides his lips over mine, savoring, and for a flash I can see how he'd undress me, run his hands down my skin, kiss me all over—sensually, seductively, as if I'm the treat he's been waiting patiently to eat. His hand runs up the bare skin of my arm, leaving a trail of goosebumps in its wake. He reaches my shoulder, gliding over the curve and up my neck.

I shiver. Oh God, how I shiver from his touch. Then his fingers dive into my hair at the nape of my neck, and he holds me as he kisses more deeply. I moan into his mouth, my body turning to jelly under his touch.

He stops, and I catch my breath, blinking. He reaches for his wallet and grabs several bills, tossing them on the table. "Want to get out of here?"

I don't know where we're going but the only answer is yes.

And *here* turns out to be the lobby. His eyes stray to the elevators, then the front desk, then me.

He raises one eyebrow. "I love a well-made bed. Do you?"

Chapter Fifteen

Dylan

She falls back on the bed once more. Just like she did the first time we entered room 521. "Yes, that's what I was thinking when you showed off the bed's best features the other day," I tell her, my voice huskier than it's been before.

"What are the bed's best features?"

"You on it. But ideally, undressed."

She tugs at the hem of her skirt, her eyelashes fluttering, saying *come and get it*.

I offer a hand, tug her up, and unzip the dress. "Just so you know, the sound of the metal teeth separating turns me on."

"Is that so?"

"Yes," I say, pressing my hard-on against her hip. "Since it means you'll be naked soon."

She moans, and I push against her. "I wanted to take your clothes off so badly the other day," I mutter.

"The thought might have crossed my mind," she says, and she's wearing this sexy grin, but she also seems more relaxed than she has before. As if she's letting go. Giving in to us.

It's a look she wears well.

I push the shoulder straps down her arms and watch as the dress falls to the floor, pooling in a silky blue pile on the plush carpet. She wears a matching bra and panties—light blue with a butterfly in the middle of the cups. "Did you...?"

I'm not sure if I should finish the thought. It's too presumptuous. *Did you wear this for me?* Yet I know the saying—if her bra and panties match, you didn't make the decision to have sex. She did. But this is Evie. She probably matches every day.

"Yes, I wore them for you. Do you like?"

"I fucking love them, and I love that answer, too," I say, and my hands are on her breasts in seconds. I groan my appreciation as I cup her tits through the lace, and she gasps. I run my hands around to her back, unhooking the bra, and gently tossing it on the bed.

And then I step back, admiring the view. "Jesus. You're so gorgeous."

She lifts her hands to my hair. "So are you."

I run my fingers from her breasts, to her belly, to her hips. "So unbelievably gorgeous."

She shudders as I touch her, then bites her lip, as if she's holding something in. I tuck a finger under her chin, lift her face to meet my eyes. "What is it?"

She angles her hips closer, pushing against my pelvis, rubbing against my hard-on. A sexy, needy sigh greets my ears. She bites her lip again.

"Just tell me, Evie. What is it?"

She nibbles on my earlobe and whispers, "I'd really like you to be inside me right now."

I groan so fucking loudly. "That's the hottest thing anyone's ever said to me," I say, and work on the buttons on my shirt as her hands expertly undo the button on my jeans.

Soon, my shirt is off, and she whistles her appreciation.

"Why, thank you," I say playfully.

"I want to nibble you all over," she says as she drags her nails down my pecs. "But I also really want this."

She pushes my jeans down my hips, and I help her along, the rest of my clothes landing in a pile on the floor.

"Can I touch?"

"I was hoping you would," I say, deadpan, and she wraps a soft hand around my cock, and my body does its best imitation of a forest fire.

Holy fuck.

Evie's touching my dick, and it's extraordinary. This woman I never thought I'd fall for has her hands on my second-favorite organ, with the brain always getting top billing.

"Too bad you're still wearing these pesky panties. But fortunately, I can solve that."

I tug them down, and when they're off I want to sing *hallelujah*. She's so pretty everywhere. Every inch of her body. Her soft, pale skin. Her small, perky breasts. Her trim waist, and this sexy blond landing strip I'd like to spend time getting to know tonight.

I bend to my jeans to grab a condom from my wallet. Then I toss it on the bed, and lower her to the covers. "I promise I'll be inside you in like ten seconds, but I need to do one thing first."

"What's that?" she whispers.

I take off my glasses, and set them on the nightstand. "That. And now this." I return to her, spread her legs, and my mouth fucking waters. Jesus. She's glistening. I bring my face between her thighs, and I lick.

She arches into me instantly, as she gasps, "Oh God."

I moan as I lick her, and her wetness spreads all over my tongue, my lips, my chin.

"But I want you inside me," she mutters as her fingers thread through my hair, and she tugs me closer, then rocks up against me.

And it doesn't take long.

Not long at all.

Thirty seconds, maybe a minute, and Evie is moaning my name over and over. She curls her hands tighter around my head, and digs her nails in. I swear they're clawing into my skull, and I love it. I love this wild, greedy, needy side of her.

She lets her knees fall open more, and she's spread for me on the hotel bed. Wide open and wanton, her back bowed, her hips bucking, until she cries out, "Oh my God."

And that's all she says. The rest is noise—noises that make me ache for her. Moans and groans and incoherent sounds as she comes on my mouth, a delicious feast of sensual woman.

I move up, wiping a hand across my mouth, and grab the condom. She's still sighing in pleasure as I open the wrapper and roll the condom down my hard length.

Her eyes flutter open. "Hi."

"Hey."

"That was fast."

"I'll take that as a good sign." I position myself between her legs and sink inside her, her wetness gripping me as I groan, sparks flying across my body. Because…this. *Her.* "Feels so good."

"So incredibly good," she says, meeting my gaze. The look in her eyes reminds me I'm going to want to do this for a long time, for many nights, because this woman… She's the one I want.

Chapter Sixteen

Evie

It's been so long, but I don't think that's why it feels so incredibly good. Sex feels this good because it's him.

I haven't felt this way for a man in a long time. I haven't felt as if I'm falling under in ages. But I feel that with Dylan, and as he pushes deep inside me, the most intense sensations ripple through my body. Tingle all over. Desire everywhere. Wanting in every molecule.

I look at him, almost afraid of what I'll see, but it's there in his eyes. This sense that he's in this with me. That the time we've spent together has been as fantastic for him as it's been for me.

I want to say something—something about how he makes me feel. But I'm afraid if I speak, I'll say way too much. And right now, I want to feel.

As he strokes inside me, I feel so much. Every single delicious sensation tears through me. My toes curl as his hips swivel, and he pushes deeper. I run my hands up his chest, loving the feel of his smooth skin under my hands. I arch into him, and I moan so loudly as his length slides exquisitely over the most sensitive part of me. It's so good.

But...

It would be even better if I changed one thing.

"Dylan," I whisper.

"Yeah?"

"I have to tell you something."

He slows, stills. "What is it?"

I whisper like I have a dark, dirty secret. "I really like being on top."

A laugh bursts from his lips. Amused, he grabs my ass and expertly rolls us over. "I thought you were going to tell me something I didn't want to hear."

I laugh, too, as I straighten, straddling him, adjusting myself to the extraordinary feel of him deep inside me. Slowly, languidly, I roll my hips, and I moan. It's a long, delicious moan, because I love this position.

"I love this," I murmur. "I can take you so deep."

His eyes blaze with heat as his hands curl tight around my hips. His fingers dig into my bones. "Funny, I like every position with you so far."

"Ditto."

I also like that we can laugh while we screw. That we can tease as we fuck. And I like that we both know when it's time to go silent. Because as I circle my hips, there's nothing more to say. There's only the sheer honesty of this moment. When you finally give in. When you finally admit. When you finally know.

I want this man. I want him so much.

And I'm having him.

I ride him as the pleasure rises inside me. I find my rhythm as my muscles tighten. My hands push hard against his chest as heat coils low in my belly, then lower still, until all this desire bursts inside me.

And I'm coming.

And crying out.

Saying his name.

Collapsing onto him, and he's right here with me, following me as he groans my name in my ear, joining me on the other side.

* * * *

Dylan brushes his fingertips along my arm. "I wasn't sure I liked you."

I swat his chest. "Your pillow talk is amazing."

He laughs and nibbles on my shoulder. "I mean it."

I roll my eyes. "And I doubly mean it now about your pillow talk."

He tugs me closer, wrapping an arm around me. "I thought we'd be too different. That's what I mean."

"I know. I thought that, too."

He lifts my hand, brings my fingers to his mouth, and presses kisses to my knuckles. "But then I got to know you."

"And you realized you really didn't like me still?" I tease.

He laughs and grabs me, pulling me closer. "Who's the difficult one now?"

I laugh. "I have no idea what you're talking about."

He presses a kiss to my lips, and even though he sent me soaring twenty minutes ago, I'm ready to go again. "By the way, did we break your third-date rule about sleeping together?" he asks.

"Did tonight seem like a first date?"

He shakes his head. "Technically it wasn't even an official date."

"Then we've botched everything."

He laughs. "But seriously, it feels like our fourth, to be honest."

I nod, smiling. "It kind of does. So we're right on track then, since my rule is wait until *after* the third date. But I also think the third time might be a charm, so we should do it a second and third time."

"I'm game."

This time he puts me on all fours and takes me hard, and I couldn't be happier, because sometimes a hard-working city girl needs to be fucked harder at night.

And this man, that's what he does to me, making me come in under three minutes.

It seems he's quite good at that.

* * * *

My phone beeps. One of those oh-so-innocent bell sounds. An I-couldn't-possibly-bother-you-so-I-sound-like-a-sweet-little-ding.

I glance at Dylan. He's sleeping like a rock.

I grab my phone and unlock the screen.

A text from Olivia glares at me. *"What's the name of the nail polish? I forgot! Also, I'm going wedding dress shopping soon. Want to come?"*

My stomach churns.

I love dress shopping.

I do, I do, I do.

But I'm naked in bed with her brother, and something feels wrong about replying to this message.

I click to my email and see if there are any work fires I need to extinguish.

The first email is from the athletic woman at the ad agency. I sent her a note a few days ago, asking if she might be interested in a date with a client.

Hi Evie! I received your email. So good to hear from you! I'm doing well and working hard, and I'm thrilled you thought of me. I'm out of town for work but would love to hear more about this guy. So hard to meet a smart, successful, good-looking one these days, who's also honest!

And the guilt triples. I'm screwing my friend's brother, and I'm skimming off the top.

At least I haven't taken his money yet.

Right now, though, I need to fix this problem.

Gently, I brush Dylan's shoulder. He rolls to his side. "Dylan," I whisper.

No response.

"Dylan," I say at a normal volume.

He snores louder.

I sigh heavily, swing my feet out of bed, and rise. After I pee, wash my face, and brush my teeth, I return to the room, expecting to find him awake.

But he's pulled a pillow over his head, and he's nowhere near opening his eyes. My chest aches as I stare at him. I want to run my fingers through his hair. I want to pepper kisses on his cheek. I want to talk to him, laugh with him, spend the whole entire day with him.

Somehow, some way, this handsome pain-in-the-butt man has worked his way into my heart.

And that means I have to deal with the consequences.

I grab the hotel stationery and dash off a note. Then I leave.

Chapter Seventeen

Dylan

The air conditioner hums gently. I rub my eyes, then reach for Evie. The sheets are empty. I blink, sit up, grab my glasses from the nightstand. The curtains are closed, and the clock flashes ten thirty at me.

Holy shit.

I slept in like I haven't done in ages.

"Hey," I call out in case she's in the bathroom. But when I get out of bed, turn on the light, and pad around the corner, there's no sign of the woman I spent the night with. I return to the bed, picking up my clothes along the way, and tugging on my boxer briefs. Then I notice a sheet of white paper by the TV.

My shoulders sag, and my chest feels hollow before I pick it up. But I swallow hard, steeling for the worst.

Especially since it starts with *Dear Dylan*. Who starts letters that way that don't end in bad news?

I had an amazing time with you. Everything has been so unexpected, and unexpectedly wonderful. But I can't work with you anymore, and I feel terrible that I broke the cardinal rule of being a matchmaker.

I will call you later.

Evie

I take a deep breath, drag a hand through my hair, and decide it's time to call a translator. I don't know what the hell this means.

Mia answers on the first ring. "Hey there, hot stuff."

"Hey. Are you free?"

"Free for lunch? No. I'm just finishing brunch with your sister. Free for you to take me for A, coffee, or B, mystery shopping, yes."

"My sister?"

"Duh. We've become friends."

"I knew that, but I didn't realize you were brunch friends."

"We are totally brunch friends. After I hung out with her at one of Chase's Scrabble parties, we both realized we had brothers who drove us crazy."

I laugh. "Chase and Max definitely can drive a sister crazy. Anyway, I don't want to interrupt your brunch. But sure, I'll choose B—mystery shopping with you."

"Great. I'm paying the bill. Good thing you called now. We instituted a cell phone-free brunch, and I literally just turned my phone back on."

* * * *

At the bath and beauty products store, Mia hands me a body wash with the name Strawberry Fields Forever. "Would you buy this for a woman?"

I sneer at the pink Strawberry Shortcake-style branding. "No."

"Now smell it."

I unscrew the cap, and I'm surprised at the light and fresh strawberry scent. I shrug. "Cheesy branding. Nice smell," I say, and Mia says thank you.

She runs a cruelty-free beauty products company on the West Coast, and she's enlisted my help from time to time when she's in town to give feedback on what a guy would buy for a girl. Now that I've given some, I figure it's time to ask her advice.

"So…I need your advice on a situation."

"Bet it all on black."

"Ha ha."

"Anyway, tell me what's up."

I lean against the shelf and give her the quick download. We hung out, I found myself liking her, we got it on, she took off with a note, yada, yada, yada.

Mia's eyes widen with each line, and when I hit the part about the hotel room—no NSFW details, of course—she shoves my shoulder. "You dog."

"I like dogs, so I'll take that as a compliment. But then she left a note and I don't know what to do."

She arches a brow. "What did it say?"

"Something about breaking a rule as a matchmaker."

Mia bounces on her toes. She clasps her fingers tightly. She draws a sharp breath. "That means she likes you!"

"Well, I would kind of hope so, since we did get a little bit naked."

"Sounds like it was more than a little bit," Mia says out of the side of her mouth.

"Fine. It was a lot naked."

She holds up a hand. "I don't want to think about you naked. The point being, that must mean she's really into you. Did you tell her how you felt? That you're totally falling for her?"

I hem and haw. "Um."

She sighs so heavily it sounds like it has its own weight class. "Dylan," she admonishes. "You didn't tell her you're falling for her?"

I cycle back to last night and the things we said. I told her how much I wanted her. I told her I liked being with her. But did I actually give voice to the most important part of my feelings? Did I ever say out loud that I was falling hard for her?

"I don't think I did."

Mia squeezes my arm. "Do it now. Don't overthink it. She probably feels guilty that she fell for you rather than found you a match. Let her know you fell for her, too. That you're in it together."

I have a lot of work ahead of me to achieve that goal. To be in it together. Time to start.

Chapter Eighteen

Evie

Olivia isn't home.

Olivia hasn't answered her phone.

Olivia isn't where I need her to be, and I'm standing in front of her brownstone, wishing her fiancé had installed a microchip in her, like she was a little beagle, and that Dylan was using his pet tracker on her.

Wait. That's a terrible thought.

I don't really want Olivia microchipped.

I do want to find my friend. As I wait on the stoop to her home, freshly showered and wearing a peach sundress, I do what any woman would do in this situation.

I dial her number every ten seconds, in between checking Pinterest for vintage clothing inspiration.

I try her number for the 417th time, cursing once more when it goes to voicemail. "Where are you?" I mutter.

"Looking for me?"

I snap my gaze up and follow the voice down the street. With big Jackie O. sunglasses, Olivia strolls down the street as if she hasn't a care in the world.

"Why aren't you answering your phone when I'm having a crisis?"

"Mia and I decided to have a cell phone-free meal. We were inspired by your effort not to look at your phone while walking, and I forgot to turn it back on."

"Don't listen to me ever again," I tell her. "I needed to reach you desperately."

She reaches the stoop and yanks off her shades. "What's going on?"

I meet her eyes, and I speak the truth. "I'm a terrible friend. I'm a terrible matchmaker. I'm a terrible businessperson."

Olivia's face is crestfallen. "Oh honey. No, you're not. What's wrong?" She wraps an arm around me. "Come inside."

A minute later, I flop down on her couch, drop my head in my hands, then look up. "I'm completely falling for your brother."

Her lips twitch. "Really?" Her voice is high-pitched, as if she's holding onto some possibility.

"Yes, and I'm so sorry. It's the cardinal rule of my business—don't fall for clients. And I did it. I fell for him. And I like him so much, and I can't set him up with anyone. And I had to tell you that I slept with your brother, and you're my friend, and I'm sorry."

"Sorry?" She cackles as she repeats the word.

"I mean it. I'm so sorry."

"Oh Evie, don't be sorry at all. I'm smiling. I'm laughing. I'm completely delighted."

"You are?"

"I think it's fabulous."

"You do?" I'm so confused. How can she be delighted?

She squeezes my arm. "Yes. I'm thrilled. I want you to be happy, and you have to stop apologizing because there's nothing wrong with falling for someone. You don't just have to make other people happy. You can be happy, too, and you didn't cross a line since you never set him up with anyone else."

I fidget with my watch. "Are you sure?"

"Hon, I'm positive. Stop being so hard on yourself. You fell for a client. It happens. But you did it before you went too far in the business relationship. Now, you can focus on being with him."

I draw a deep breath. "That's the thing. We're not technically together yet."

"Does he know how you feel?"

"Sort of?" I offer with a shrug.

"Let's make sure it's more than *sort of.* You helped me find the love of my life. Now it's my turn to help you."

* * * *

I walk home, weighing what to say and how to say it. When I reach my apartment in Chelsea, a plan is fully formed. It's simple but direct, and I think that's what I need at this point. Once inside, I sit down at my desk, grab a fresh sheet of paper, and write another note.

I head to the bathroom, check my reflection, freshen up my makeup, fluff out my hair, and call Dylan.

"Hey you," he says when he answers, and the way those two words sound melts me.

I like this guy so much. "Hey."

"How are you?"

"I'm good. I was hoping to see you," I say as nerves flutter inside me.

"I was hoping to see you." He takes a beat. "In about five minutes."

I startle. "What?"

"I'm in your neighborhood. Can I come over?"

"Yes." The word comes out as if it's the only thing I've ever wanted to say to him.

When he arrives, and I buzz him in, I peer down the hall. As soon as he rounds the top of the stairs, my heart flip-flops in my chest, like a fish on the shore. I place a hand on my belly, as if that'll calm me down, but I'm not calm, nor cool, nor collected. Because he's here. Striding toward me, carrying a cute little pink shopping bag with a bow on it. He wears jeans and a gray T-shirt that fits him well, showing off those arms that caged me in last night, that spread me open, that held me close. And those eyes are smiling, but I also see the nerves in them.

That's what turns me inside out with hope. He's as nervous as I am.

"Hi." My voice is breathy. "Want to come in?"

"I'd love to."

I hold open the door, and he steps inside my one-bedroom for the first time. It's light and airy, with three cool white walls and a sky blue one. The curtains flutter in the summer breeze. Magazines and books are stacked neatly on my silver coffee table, alongside a vase of blue irises.

"You are a neat freak," he says.

I smile, owning it. I show him to the dove gray couch, and we sit. I grab the letter. "I wrote you a letter," I blurt.

"I bought you some gifts."

I laugh, and he does, too.

"Jesus, are we both dorks?" he asks.

"Maybe," I say with a laugh.

He sets down the bag on the coffee table, then meets my eyes. He parts his lips to speak, then mutters *fuck it*. He cups my face in his hands and dips his mouth to mine. We kiss, and I feel as if it's been days rather than hours. He slides his lips over mine like he wants to do it again and again, for a long time. It's dreamy and tingly, sexy and hot at the same damn time.

When we separate, he breathes out hard as he holds up a finger, the sign to wait. "First, forgive me. It's going to be very hard for me to not kiss you right away when I see you."

A smile spreads on me. "Is that so?"

"Because I'd really like to keep kissing you. And to keep seeing you. And to keep dating you." He runs a hand through my hair, and I lean into it. "I'm not interested in anyone else. I'm falling so hard for you."

I squeak.

Yep.

I freaking squeak as my heart shimmies up my chest and does a jig. "I'm falling for you, Dylan," I say, and then it's my turn to stop resisting. I run my finger over his top lip, and I dive in for a quick and passionate kiss. He pulls away and reaches for the bag. "I have some gifts that I hope will show you how I feel."

I rub my hands together. "I love gifts."

"I figured you did."

He reaches into the bag and hands me a cup of boba tea. "I picked this up a few minutes ago. This is because I want to experience new things with you, like this tea that I suddenly like a lot."

He hands it to me, and I take a sip. It sends a dose of happiness through me. I give it back to him and say, "You have some now."

He leans into the straw and sucks, his eyebrows wiggling in delight. Then his hand goes fishing again, and he takes out a jar of spicy salsa. "This is because there's no one I'd rather take out for cheap tacos or for fancy sushi, for that matter."

"I want to be the one you take out. For both," I say.

One more dip inside, and he grabs something black. A swath of fabric. I arch a brow in question as he hands me the material. Yoga pants.

"This is because I like you so much I'd tolerate yoga to be with you," he says. "Also because your ass looks spectacular in yoga pants."

I shift my shoulder toward him flirtily. "Yours looks great in gym shorts."

He reaches for my hand and threads his fingers through mine. Sparks spread in my body, and it feels so damn good. "I want you to match me with you."

And my heart skips out of my chest, flinging itself at him.

But I have things to say, too. "I left quickly this morning because I felt like I was taking something away from my clients because of how I want you. But even if I feel guilty, it's not changing how I feel for you."

His smile is beautiful as he squeezes my hand. "Good."

"You have to know I tried to do my job. I tried to find someone for you." I raise my chin, ready to deliver my news. "And I think I have."

"What?" The look on his face is pure confusion.

"I reached out to a matchmaker," I say, in a happy, upbeat tone.

He furrows his brow. "Why would you do that?"

"It's a woman I know. A friendly competitor."

He drops my hand. "I don't get it."

"I told her what I'm looking for." I hand him the letter.

Chapter Nineteen

Dylan

I unfold her note.

When I read it, there's no poker face on earth that can contain the grin I feel inside.

> **Woman seeking man:**
> **Fun, successful, slightly competitive, bargain-hunting, boba tea-loving woman who runs her own business seeks her very own pain-in-the-butt, handsome-as-hell, brainy guy who wears panty-melting glasses, has hair she wants to run her hands through, loves to play the kinds of games that should be played, and who makes her feel like he only has eyes for her. She wants them to share all the good things, from new experiences, to discovering the city, to dining cheap and dining expensively, to hot nights and fun days and all the adventures of this world together.**

I place the paper on the table. "I think you found a buyer, Evie."

She smiles so brightly it makes my heart thump harder. "You have to know I didn't think I wanted a relationship. I didn't think the time was right," she says, curling her hand over my shoulder.

"But I wormed my way into your heart."

"You're persistent."

I pump a fist. "And not taking no for an answer paid off."

"It did. I didn't expect to want this or you. But I do. I want you so much. I want to be the one you choose."

I shake my head, amused that she'd think there's any choice for me but her. I bring my forehead to hers and say what I didn't say last night. "You're who I want."

"What would you say about a second date then?"

I raise a brow. "Second? I say it's the fifth."

"Oh well, if it's the fifth, we can go to my bedroom right now."

"Only if I can do unspeakable things to you on your pristinely made bed."

"I'd expect nothing less."

She's already exceeded all my expectations, and I have a feeling that's how it's going to be with her. Can't say I mind that at all.

Chapter Twenty

Mia

At a bar in Midtown called Speakeasy, Mia nursed a Purple Snow Globe as she waited for Olivia, her mind wandering to her friend Dylan and the new woman in his life. Evie was a fun, smart, lovely lady. Evie also happened to have a brother, who Mia had grown quite fond of.

An image of Patrick flashed before her eyes—tall, broad, strong, and with a smile she couldn't look away from. From the first time she'd met him at her brother Max's apartment, she'd found him devilishly attractive. She craved him so much. More than he could know. But there were hurdles.

But there had been hurdles for Dylan and Evie, and they were on the path to crossing them. Mia had high hopes for the two of them.

After all, that was why she and Olivia were meeting tonight, once again. At last, they could celebrate their efforts.

When Olivia arrived, she did a little victory dance, hands in the air, hips shaking, brown hair shimmering. Mia joined her, then they smacked palms.

"We did it," Olivia said.

Mia raised her glass. "We are awesome matchmakers."

"Sometimes people don't know what's in front of them until their friends push them together."

"It's a good thing they both have such great friends."

Epilogue

Indeed, some things are not what they seem. From time to time, the matchmaker gets matched. By her friends.

Because sometimes, a man and a woman can't see how very good they'd be together. They only see differences, even if they've both been trained to look beneath the surface. But people are people, and don't always peer closely when it comes to themselves. Yet their friends could see. Their friends could tell. And their friends knew that Evie and Dylan only needed a nudge in the right direction to come together.

That ad Dylan placed? Mia was glad he ran it, since it allowed her to tell Olivia, so Olivia could show it to Evie. For Olivia knew that once Evie saw it, she would insist on helping. And once she helped, how could she do anything but fall for the man both their friends knew was right for her? The matchmaker and the hot nerd simply needed to spend time together to see that they wanted new experiences, that they both were competitive in their own ways, and that they loved to uncover the city.

When the two seemed resistant to a match, that was when Mia and Olivia called in reinforcement. That hike in the woods between brother and sister? Mia was the one who coaxed Patrick into asking those questions of his sister, hoping the questions would encourage Evie to see Dylan in a new way.

And she did. Dylan saw Evie in a new way, too, as they discovered more about each other and all the things they loved. But in the end, what they loved most was each other.

For this isn't a story of how opposites attract. It's a story of friendships. And how sometimes, our friends can see what we need the most.

As for Dylan and Evie, when we last left them they were falling in love. And right now? Let's see where they are, shall we?

Another Epilogue

Two weeks later

Dylan

I shake my head. She's wrong. So wrong. "That movie was awesome. I seriously can't believe you didn't like it," I say as we leave the theater in Chelsea.

"It was unnecessarily long, it was unnecessarily violent, and there wasn't enough humor."

"But the car chases. Didn't you at least like the car chases?"

She stops in her tracks and stares at me. "Did I at least like the car chases?" She asks the question as if it's an incredulous notion. "Who cares when the rest of it was painful to watch?"

"You'd probably rather see a movie where there's some couple walking down the street in New York City, and the dude sees flowers in a shop and says they remind him of her, and then he tells her how he feels."

Her blue eyes sparkle, and she grins. "See? That sounds great. I'd like to see that."

I drape an arm around her and tug her close. "We'll see that next time," I say softly.

"And we'll debate it, too, I have no doubt."

"Nor do I."

We don't always see eye to eye, and that's okay. Because we talk. We find ways to connect even when we don't agree. It's kind of funny how I didn't see what was right in front of me all along. But thanks to my sister and my friend—who did admit that they maybe, possibly, okay fine, totally engineered the whole matchmaking thing to get us together—I'm with the woman I adore.

As we round the corner past a flower shop with a window full of blue irises, I'm struck with the thought of how much they remind me of Evie's eyes.

Eyes I love looking into.

Eyes I love getting lost in.

I stop, grab her hand, and yank her close to me. "Hey you," I whisper.

"Hey you."

"Want to know something?"

"I do."

My eyes drift briefly to the flowers. "We're outside a flower shop."

"You don't say."

I rub my thumb along her cheek. There are no nerves inside me this time. Only certainty. "I'm in love with you."

She leans into my hand. "I'm so in love with you."

And that's something we see eye to eye on, and I know we will for a long, long time.

Like, maybe, for happily ever after.

THE END

* * * *

Also from 1001 Dark Nights and Lauren Blakely, discover The Only One.

Big Rock Character Connections

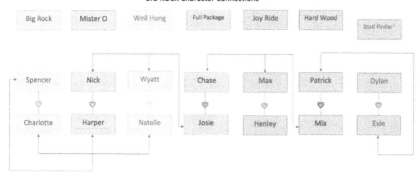

BIG ROCK Character Connections

Big Rock	Mister O	Well Hung	Full Package	Joy Ride	Hard Wood	Stud Finder*

Spencer	Nick	Wyatt	Chase	Max	Patrick	Dylan
Charlotte	Harper	Natalie	Josie	Henley	Mia	Evie

*Stud Finder is a standalone, dual-POV novella that links characters from The Knocked Up Plan with the Big Rock books and does not need to be read in any order.

→ Solid line denotes siblings

Big Rock Series Character Connections

Big Rock Series Character Connections

Siblings/Family Name	Couples	Friends
Holiday	**Big Rock**	Spencer/Nick
Spencer (Big Rock)	Spencer	Wyatt/Chase
Harper (Mister O)	Charlotte	Natalie/Josie
		Max/Patrick
Hammer	**Mister O**	
Nick (Mister O)	Harper	
Wyatt (Well Hung)	Nick	
Josie (Full Package)		
	Well Hung	
Summers	Wyatt	
Chase (Full Package)	Natalie	
Max (Joy Ride)		
Mia (Hard Wood)	**Full Package**	
	Josie	
Rhodes	Chase	
Charlotte (Big Rock)		
Natalie (Well Hung)	**Joy Ride**	
	Max	
Milligan	Henley	
Patrick (Hard Wood)		
Evie (Stud Finder novella)	**Hard Wood**	
	Mia	
	Patrick	

Special thanks to Dena Marie for creating The Big Rock character map and to Melissa Buyikian for creating the character lists.

Sign up for the 1001 Dark Nights Newsletter
and be entered to win a Tiffany Key necklace.

There's a contest every month!

Go to www.1001DarkNights.com to subscribe.

As a bonus, all subscribers will receive a free
1001 Dark Nights story
The First Night
by Lexi Blake & M.J. Rose

Discover 1001 Dark Nights Collection Four

Go to www.1001DarkNights.com for more information.

ROCK CHICK REAWAKENING by Kristen Ashley
A Rock Chick Novella

ADORING INK by Carrie Ann Ryan
A Montgomery Ink Novella

SWEET RIVALRY by K. Bromberg

SHADE'S LADY by Joanna Wylde
A Reapers MC Novella

RAZR by Larissa Ione
A Demonica Underworld Novella

ARRANGED by Lexi Blake
A Masters and Mercenaries Novella

TANGLED by Rebecca Zanetti
A Dark Protectors Novella

HOLD ME by J. Kenner
A Stark Ever After Novella

SOMEHOW, SOME WAY by Jennifer Probst
A Billionaire Builders Novella

TOO CLOSE TO CALL by Tessa Bailey
A Romancing the Clarksons Novella

HUNTED by Elisabeth Naughton
An Eternal Guardians Novella

EYES ON YOU by Laura Kaye
A Blasphemy Novella

BLADE by Alexandra Ivy/Laura Wright
A Bayou Heat Novella

DRAGON BURN by Donna Grant
A Dark Kings Novella

TRIPPED OUT by Lorelei James
A Blacktop Cowboys® Novella

STUD FINDER by Lauren Blakely

MIDNIGHT UNLEASHED by Lara Adrian
A Midnight Breed Novella

HALLOW BE THE HAUNT by Heather Graham
A Krewe of Hunters Novella

DIRTY FILTHY FIX by Laurelin Paige
A Fixed Novella

THE BED MATE by Kendall Ryan
A Room Mate Novella

NIGHT GAMES by CD Reiss
A Games Novella

NO RESERVATIONS by Kristen Proby
A Fusion Novella

DAWN OF SURRENDER by Liliana Hart
A MacKenzie Family Novella

Discover 1001 Dark Nights Collection One

Go to www.1001DarkNights.com for more information.

FOREVER WICKED by Shayla Black
CRIMSON TWILIGHT by Heather Graham
CAPTURED IN SURRENDER by Liliana Hart
SILENT BITE: A SCANGUARDS WEDDING by Tina Folsom
DUNGEON GAMES by Lexi Blake
AZAGOTH by Larissa Ione
NEED YOU NOW by Lisa Renee Jones
SHOW ME, BABY by Cherise Sinclair
ROPED IN by Lorelei James
TEMPTED BY MIDNIGHT by Lara Adrian
THE FLAME by Christopher Rice
CARESS OF DARKNESS by Julie Kenner

Also from 1001 Dark Nights

TAME ME by J. Kenner

Discover 1001 Dark Nights Collection Two

Go to www.1001DarkNights.com for more information.

WICKED WOLF by Carrie Ann Ryan
WHEN IRISH EYES ARE HAUNTING by Heather Graham
EASY WITH YOU by Kristen Proby
MASTER OF FREEDOM by Cherise Sinclair
CARESS OF PLEASURE by Julie Kenner
ADORED by Lexi Blake
HADES by Larissa Ione
RAVAGED by Elisabeth Naughton
DREAM OF YOU by Jennifer L. Armentrout
STRIPPED DOWN by Lorelei James
RAGE/KILLIAN by Alexandra Ivy/Laura Wright
DRAGON KING by Donna Grant
PURE WICKED by Shayla Black
HARD AS STEEL by Laura Kaye
STROKE OF MIDNIGHT by Lara Adrian
ALL HALLOWS EVE by Heather Graham
KISS THE FLAME by Christopher Rice
DARING HER LOVE by Melissa Foster
TEASED by Rebecca Zanetti
THE PROMISE OF SURRENDER by Liliana Hart

Also from 1001 Dark Nights

THE SURRENDER GATE By Christopher Rice
SERVICING THE TARGET By Cherise Sinclair

Discover 1001 Dark Nights Collection Three

Go to www.1001DarkNights.com for more information.

About Lauren Blakely

A #1 New York Times Bestselling author, Lauren Blakely is known for her contemporary romance style that's hot, sweet and sexy. She lives in California with her family and has plotted entire novels while walking her dogs. With fourteen New York Times bestsellers, her titles have appeared on the New York Times, USA Today, and Wall Street Journal Bestseller Lists more than 85 times, and she's sold more than 2 million books. She enjoys cake, comedy and cat videos. To receive an email when Lauren releases a new book, sign up for her newsletter here!

Discover More Lauren Blakely

The Only One
A One Love Novella
By Lauren Blakely

From *New York Times* bestselling author Lauren Blakely...

Let's say there was this guy. And he gave you the most mind-blowing night of sex in your life. And you never saw him again.

Until ten years later.

Now, it turns out he's the ONLY ONE in all of Manhattan whose restaurant is available for my charity's event.

The trouble is, he doesn't recognize me.

* * * *

This woman I'm working with is so damn alluring. The first time I set eyes on her, I'm captivated and I can't get her out of my mind. Even if it's risky to tango with someone I'm working with, she's a risk I'm willing to take.

The trouble is, she won't give me the time of day.

But I'm determined to change that.

Hard Wood
By Lauren Blakely
Coming October 23, 2017

Wondering about Evie's brother Patrick? And Dylan's friend Mia? Their romance is Hard Wood, releasing in October! A sneak peek follows.

Women often say a good man is hard to find. And a hard man is even better.

That's why I'm quite a catch— good, hard, loaded, and wait for it… I'm ready to settle down too. But the woman I want to pitch my tent with lives clear across the country. Neither of us wants to get lost in those woods. All I have to do is resist her for the week she's in town.

I try. I swear I try. But yeah, that doesn't work out.

And after one fantastic night with my good friend Mia, I'm ready to give her years of nights under the stars. What's a few thousand miles when love's involved? But there's a hitch in my plans—she just hired my adventure tour company. If there's one thing I'm committed to, it's running a squeaky clean business. Number one on my list of iron-clad rules?

Don't screw your customers.

But what's a guy to do when she's so hard to resist? How hard can it be to keep our hands off each other for a quick group tour down the hills and over the trails? I'm about to find out, and I have a feeling I'm going to need a new badge of honor because things are about to get very hard in the woods.

* * * *

Prologue

By now, most women have met the half dozen or so basic types of men in the world.

Just to be sure, though, let's review the lineup.

First, there's the too-cool-for-school playboy who solemnly swears he'll never settle down. Next to him in the modern-day parade of dudes is the Grouchy McGrouch Pants. This surly bearded guy is a softie beneath the dickhead exterior he shows to the world, along with his beanie cap. By his side is the guarded businessman in his three-piece suit, housing deep, dark secrets that only one woman can unlock. We have other roles in Guy Central Casting—the lumbersexual, the groomed father, the citified pretty boy, the hot nerd, and the bad boy with a heart of gold.

Trust me when I say the ladies of the world have heard their stories.

I know that because I've fucking heard them. I've heard them from the guys, and I've heard them from the gals. When you take people out of their comfort zone and into the woods, they tend to tell you everything—every sordid detail. I'm honestly kind of amazed that men and women, women and women, and men and men get together at all. There's so much baggage going around, it's like a goddamn virus.

As for me?

I'm simple. I travel light. I don't bring luggage to the table. I hoist my backpack and I'm ready to go.

I'm a man of many skills. Give me a battery and I'll start a campfire. Show me an old phone and I'll make a compass. I'm the guy who knows how to get out of jams. I can fix a tire, repair a sink, gut a fish, pick a lock, survive a bear attack—I've been there, done that, and have the merit badges to prove it.

Not gonna lie. Women do tend to like a guy who can get shit done without bitching about it. That's why I've had a nice run of luck with the ladies. But I'm not looking just to get lucky anymore.

I'm ready for a whole lot more.

I'd like to think that makes me the good guy with all the skills when we're talking about types. I'm the unicorn, and I'm not just talking about the length of my horn, if you catch my drift.

I'm the guy who's fit, successful, baggage-fucking-free, and—wait for it—ready to settle down.

Just call me a four-leaf clover.

The trouble is the woman I want is off-limits. She's my best friend's sister. But don't worry. That's not the issue. My buddy is a cool cat, and he has no problem with the fact that I've got it bad for his little sis.

The problem is something else entirely, and I have the next week before she leaves town again to fix it. This is where all my life-hacking skills will have to come into play.

Let's do this.

* * * *

Chapter One

Human beings tend to overthink all sorts of stuff, but a lot of our quandaries are pretty basic. You're either going out to dinner at the new Italian joint, or you're staying home to make a turkey sandwich. You're doing the laundry so you have a fresh shirt to wear, or you're sniffing the hamper, hunting for an old-but-good-enough-ie. You either carve out the time to run five miles, or you watch another ten episodes of *Breaking Bad.*

For the record, the answers are Italian, wash on hot, and lace up.

I take the same straightforward approach to the current black-and-white question posed to me by Camilla Montes, the local Channel Ten morning news anchor.

"Patrick, how will our viewers know if Fluffy wants to go for a hike?" she asks in that perfectly modulated TV reporter voice that matches her coiffed black hair.

"If you're wondering if Tiger, Tom, or Tabby is ready to become an adventure cat, there's a simple litmus test any pet owner can conduct." I sit on the couch across from her and run a hand down Zeus's back. He arches into my palm and rumbles, his purr so loud he could land a career in the cat sound-effects business. *Showoff.* But in his defense, if I possessed an Al Green-style purr, I'd make sure the ladies heard it all the time too. "I like to call it the drag or no-drag cat."

"Interesting. Tell us more," she says, her voice dripping with curiosity.

"Your cat either willingly lets you put a leash around his furry neck, or he turns into putty when you harness him, and you wind up dragging his feline butt across the floor." I mime tugging a gone-limp cat on a leash.

"That does make it crystal clear," Camilla says, flashing her practiced grin, then she points a polished fingernail at me. "But how did you even know to try with Zeus? Did you simply want a famous hiking partner, or did he insist on it?"

"I listened to the cat." I lean forward, parking one hand on my knee where my cargo shorts end, since the station likes me to dress like an REI model for my segments on Tips and Tricks for Enjoying the Great Outdoors. "His behavior told me he might be willing. For instance, one time, I headed down to the hallway to drop the trash in the chute, and Zeus followed me out the door of the apartment, staying by my side the whole time." I lower my voice, cup the side of my mouth, and speak in a stage whisper. "And I don't think it was *only* because there was leftover salmon in the trash."

Camilla laughs.

"Salmon aside, he exhibited this inquisitive behavior often, and that's when I decided to give a leash and harness a whirl."

"And now he's become the Hiking Tomcat." She gestures grandly to my long-haired cat, who's lounging next to me, his white gloved paws folded in front of his chest, and a look of satisfaction on his furry face. I swear this dude is such a ham. He was born for the cameras. "Can you show our viewers how a cat who likes to go for hikes will handle being harnessed?"

"Why, I thought you'd never ask," I say as I stand, grab the leash and harness from the couch, and pat my leg.

Zeus stretches, slinks down the side of the couch, and gazes up at me.

"Want to go for a hike?"

His tail swishes back and forth.

Look, I'm not claiming he understands English. He's a cat, after all, not some kind of Cesar Milan-trained dog. But Zeus knows the drill, and the leash is dangling in my hand. He stretches his neck out, almost as if he's inviting me to put the red hiking harness over his head. I slide it on and clip a leash to the end. Zeus struts a few feet.

Camila's smile beams as brightly as the TV lights blasting from above. "There you go."

"Would you like to walk him, Camilla?"

Her glossy red lips part in a wide grin. "I would love to walk this

Internet superstar."

I place a finger to my lips. "Shhh. We don't want his fame to go to his head."

"If he only knew how purr-fectly popular he is." Camilla takes the leash and walks Zeus around the set. "We brought in something to simulate the conditions on the trails."

Camilla escorts my boy to some fake rocks set up for this demo while the on-air screen shows an Internet video I've shot of Zeus clambering up a hill on a nearby trail. When they reach the rocks, the shot returns to Camilla, walking alongside in heels as Zeus scurries up the rocks and then down the other side. Note to self—score this cat some commercial work and see if we can retire on Friskies royalties.

But then, I've no interest in slowing down. My life is the textbook definition of *so fucking good*. My business is thriving, my family is healthy and happy, and my friends are settling down. There's only one thing I long for more of. Well, not a thing. More like a lovely, captivating, I-just-click-with-her *someone*.

But now's not the time to dwell on a certain woman.

Camilla returns to her blue chair, and I park myself on the couch again, alongside my loyal companion. I spend the next forty-five seconds reviewing trail safety for those who walk with their cats. After all, hiking with a feline is not for the faint of heart. People with dogs have no idea how easy they have it. Hiking with a feline is a whole other kettle of fish, but well worth it for the photos alone. We're talking unexpected goldmine. When my sister, Evie, plunked this cat on my doorstep and begged me to give him a home, I had no idea he'd turn out to be, one, totally cool, and two, the best marketing ever for my adventure tour company.

When the segment ends, Camilla thanks me and cuts to a commercial. "See you again next week, Patrick. I've been thinking we could do a piece on first aid in the woods."

"Absolutely."

"And you know what I've been dying to have you do a segment on?"

"Whatever you want, I can do it," I say, keeping up the easygoing vibe, since that's what works best for business partners.

"What if we did a piece on how to glamp?"

I chuckle lightly, rubbing a palm across my short, neat beard. "I can do that, and I can also give you a simple trick for camping with style right now if you'd like."

Her chocolate brown eyes twinkle with excitement. "Please do."

"Do you have your phone with you?"

"Of course. It's on silent, but I'm never without my closest companion," she says, taking it from her skirt pocket, unlocking the screen, and handing it to me.

I tap a few words into the search bar, and the result I need returns quickly. I hand the phone to Camilla. "This is who you call."

Her reaction is priceless—a slow smile spreads as the name and number for the Ritz Carlton appear on her screen.

"So true. What can I say? I'm not an outdoorsy girl at all. But I love your segments. So does my new intern, Taylor," she says, lowering her voice and looking toward a bubbly blonde who's waiting to escort me from the set. Funny, since my job requires me to find my way out of pretty much anywhere on God's great green Earth. Not to mention, I've been the guest commentator for the station's Friday morning outdoors segments for a few months now. The gig has done wonders for my business, but nowhere near what Zeus has done.

Then, because I like the furry dude and I don't want to torture him—and taking a cat for a walk on the sidewalks of Manhattan is a unique and terrible form of torture—I drop Zeus into my backpack, slide the straps on, and leave the studio with the perky cheerleader girl by my side and the cat's silvery head poking out the top of the pack.

"I made s'mores the other day," Taylor offers with a big smile, her bright blue eyes meeting mine. "They were so good."

Her *so* has eight syllables and all of them drip with innuendo.

"That's great," I say, since I'm not interested in entertaining any syllables or innuendo with someone barely past puberty.

"Do you like s'mores, Patrick?"

"Who doesn't like s'mores?"

"I was wondering, though, if you might have any tips for me on how to make them. Like, how do I get the chocolate and marshmallow to *come* together perfectly." She stops at the door, leans her hip against it suggestively, and twirls a strand of her hair.

And I do believe s'mores porn is officially a thing.

Even though I pride myself on making the world's greatest version of the campfire treat, I keep my answer simple, but clear. "It's all in how long you let the ingredients *age*," I say, since Taylor is twenty, twenty-one at best. "See you next week."

I say goodbye and leave, catching a train downtown, then walking through the streets of lower Manhattan.

Do I get stares because of the cat on my back?

Hell, yeah.

Do I enjoy it?

Absolutely.

I smile and nod, giving a few salutes and a couple of *how are yous* and even a *meow* as a little kid walks by with her mom and whispers while pointing at my shoulder. As if I don't know there's a badass pussycat purring in my ear.

As I turn onto the block with my building, he's not the only one purring.

Because there, right fucking there in front of the lobby, wearing reflective sunglasses and jeans that hug her curves deliciously, is a certain woman.

Mia Summers. Tiny but mighty. A powerful sprite with wavy hair, hazel eyes, a soft heart, and a quick wit that I just dig.

I met her several months ago, and it's safe to say she's claimed center stage in my mind ever since then.

When I see Mia, when I talk to Mia, when I spend time with Mia, it confirms my belief that some things are simple.

Like whether a cat drags his whole body on the floor or he gamely trots alongside you.

It's a yes or no.

A black or white.

You're either attracted to your best friend's sister or you're not.

For the record, the answer is I am, so fucking much.

On behalf of 1001 Dark Nights,

Liz Berry and M.J. Rose would like to thank ~

Steve Berry
Doug Scofield
Kim Guidroz
Jillian Stein
InkSlinger PR
Dan Slater
Asha Hossain
Chris Graham
Pamela Jamison
Fedora Chen
Kasi Alexander
Jessica Johns
Dylan Stockton
Richard Blake
BookTrib After Dark
and Simon Lipskar

CPSIA information can be obtained
at www.ICGtesting.com
Printed in the USA
LVHW041805270220
648406LV00003B/540